KILTY MIND

KILTY SERIES: BOOK THREE

Amy Vansant

CHAPTER ONE

Two weeks ago.

She could feel him near.

Seething.

The pungent fragrance of his fury tickled her nostrils like the aroma of warm, fresh-baked bread on a Paris summer morning.

This is an angry one.

This one would leap into action with the slightest provocation. *A nudge.* She'd sit beside him. Say hello. If he proved the chatty type, maybe slip him an idea or two.

Be inspiring. That's my motto.

Making an abrupt shift to the right, she crossed the main thoroughfare of The Grove, Los Angeles' high-end outdoor shopping mall, dodging both people and swinging shopping bags.

She perched on the bench beside him.

Hello beautiful.

The man wasn't beautiful. He was short and balding with a dark swirl of comb-over attempting to hide an impressive collection of moles on his skull. One might describe him as *toady.*

Not Fiona. Like a sculptor, she saw the work of art inside the lump of clay.

She knew quite a bit about this particular lump.

Mole-headed producer Gregory Pitkin had suffered a series of flops and his wife had packed up the kids and moved to Brentwood. The rumor mill said Mrs. Pitkin had taken a lover. One with fewer spots on the cranium and some length of bone.

Most importantly, Fiona knew Gregory Pitkin lived in the fifteen-oh-one penthouse of the new Shalimar condominiums overlooking Parasol Pictures' lot.

She wanted that penthouse.

Fiona opened her purse and retrieved a compact. Powdering her nose, she made a kissy-face in the mirror to check her lipstick.

"You don't deserve this," she said, loud enough for him to hear no matter on what planet his mind might be wandering. She ran her tongue across her teeth and snapped the compact shut.

"Huh?" he said as if waking from a dream.

She put a hand on his knee and stared into his eyes.

"You don't deserve this, Gregory Pitkin. Any of it."

He swallowed. Spine straightening, he pushed aside the broken, shoulder-hunched look of a beaten man. He took a deep breath and tilted back his head, staring into the heavens as if ready to accept divine intervention.

She could *hear* the gears in his mind whirring.

Divine intervention, indeed.

Without looking at her, he stood and strode off.

A man of purpose.

A man reborn.

A man with a *mission.*

Fiona smiled.

You're welcome.

She stood and walked by two children, each grasping ice cream cones and gobbling with frenzied determination. With a toss of her head, she caught the attention of the older boy, her eyes flicking toward the younger's treat.

The older boy's gaze followed hers as if pulled on a string. His lips puckered tight, brow lowering until the space between his eyes transformed into an adorable crinkled knob of young flesh.

He slapped the cone from his brother's hand.

For a moment, it was as if time stood still.

The child's expression opened like a hibiscus in the morning sun—eyes wide, jaw slack. The ice cream arced into the air until gravity snatched it and spiked it to the ground with a *splat.*

He wailed like a racing ambulance.

Fiona walked on, chuckling.

Still got it.

CHAPTER TWO

Present Day

Chilly beneath his hospital gown, Brochan pushed open the door to the men's room and entered. The pain from the gunshot wound beneath his arm no longer nagged. He guessed it had something to do with the large needles the doctor had stuck into his flesh. Or maybe the pills they'd given him. Or maybe the additional pills he'd taken after they left the room.

If two pills made him feel good, he'd guessed six would make him feel even better. They'd told him to wait before taking more, but *how come?* It didn't make any sense. Surely the more healing magic the better. They didn't have *pills* where he'd come from—not even his most recent memory, from nineteenth-century Scotland—but he imagined the little white bullets worked akin to balls of medicinal herbs.

Whitevur. They worked. He felt pain-free and maybe a touch giddy.

He needed to be at his best.

Tonight he'd be with Catriona. Tonight he'd ask her—

Broch stopped his forward momentum. He felt the grin on his mug melting, like the gelato he'd left on the counter of his new Hollywood apartment before he understood that frozen desserts required constant cold.

In front of him in the men's room, a slight, blond man stepped toward a sink embedded in the wall.

Ah ken the back o' that scrawny man's heid.

He was sure of it. What was his name?

Pete.

Catriona called him by that name. Sometimes she called him Dr. No-See-Um.

That wee man spent a nicht wi' Catriona.

Broch felt heat rise in his cheeks—a strange mixture of anger and embarrassment. He felt much the way he had while watching Pete leave Catriona's apartment, *much too early in the morning.*

The wee man was so close now he could reach out and snap his twiggy neck. Anger bubbled in his chest as Pete struggled to unbutton his trousers.

Why had *that one* been at Catriona's apartment overnight? The Lilliputian couldn't even find his wedding tackle with both hands.

Brochan felt a growl starting in his throat.

Pete turned and Broch watched the color drain from the man's face. The doctor's eyes bugged as wide as skipping stones.

"Holy—"

Broch strode forward. "Hello, *Pete*."

"Hey, Broch, right? Did you just growl?"

Did I?

Pete stared up at him, Adam's apple bobbing. He coughed a dry, raspy honk. "Fancy meeting you here. How are you feeling? I, uh, heard you were shot helping Catriona with a job?"

"Aye. Ah ate all the pills. 'Tis all guid noo."

Pete frowned. "You ate *all* the pills?"

Broch waved away the tiny doctor's question as if he were erasing it from the world. "Nevermind that. Ah've bin meanin' tae speak tae ye—"

Pete dropped his gaze to his navel and began to rebutton his trousers. "Now isn't a great time..."

Broch laid a hand on the doctor's arm, marveling at how dainty the man's shoulder felt in his hand.

Lik' a marble ah cuid throw...

He couldn't let Pete leave yet. He needed answers. He knew Catriona wouldn't like him menacing her friend, but at the moment, he found it hard to care. He felt...*free*. Light on his feet.

"Are you okay?" asked Dr. Pete.

Broch glanced down from the spot he'd been staring at on the ceiling. The doctor peered back up at him, head tilted as if he was watching something he didn't quite understand.

Broch refocused. "Dae whit ye've come tae dae. Ah'm nae aff tae hurt ye."

With a grimace, Pete worked his way down the buttons of his pants once again and resumed waiting for his river to run.

"It's a little uncomfortable with your hand on my shoulder, big guy," he mumbled. "I didn't think I had a shy bladder but I think you've done it."

Broch removed his hand. He'd lost track of time, remembering how Catriona had yelled at him when *he'd* attempted to relieve himself in a sink. Pete, like him, didn't seem to think it should be a problem. He did like *that* about Pete.

"Catrionia tellt me nae tae dae it in a sink."

Pete's head swiveled from the death glare he'd locked on his business. "What?"

"Whit ye're daein' in that sink. She tellt me nae tae dae it."

Pete glanced down. "You mean the urinal?"

Broch blinked at him.

"You've never seen—" The corner of Pete's mouth hooked to the right as he squinted at Broch. "This is a *urinal*. You're supposed to pee in it. That's what it's for."

"It's nae a sink?"

"No."

Broch studied the urinal in front of him.

Alright then. It is an odd shape.

He lifted his hospital gown to find his own equipment and relieve the pressure on his bladder.

Pete quickly looked away. "Jeezus."

"Whit?"

"Nothing. I'm just realizing God's got a sense of humor."

"Whit's that suppose tae mean?" He looked down. "Is thare somethin' wrong wi' it?"

Pete laughed. "Wrong? No. Unless you're exhausted from carting it around all day, which I imagine is possible."

Broch squinted at him. "Yer saying it's tae big?"

"Too big—" A strange smile curled at the corner of Pete's lips. "You mean for Catriona? She hasn't, uh, tried it on for size yet?"

Broch felt his flash of anger return. "*Na.* She's a proper lassie."

Pete snorted a laugh and Broch stabbed a finger at him.

"Ye better watch yer geggie."

"My geggie?"

"Yer *mouth*. Afore ah batter it shut."

"Oh. Er, Sorry."

Broch stared down again. "Bit dae ye think... Ah, mean, is whit ye've git more tae a wummin's liking?"

Pete grimaced. "Ah. Great. Thanks for pointing out mine is *different*. Couldn't just let me pretend?"

Broch opened his mouth and then shut it. He wanted to know if everyone in modern-day had rigging like Pete, but Catriona had told him not to tell anyone about his time travel.

If she wanted Pete to know, she'd have told him herself.

The room spun a little to the left so Broch closed his eyes and shook his head to clear it.

He began to relieve himself. "Nevermind."

They fell silent as Pete found his own relief. As he did, he looked up at Broch.

"If you're asking me if carrying Thor's hammer between your legs might scare her, though... It *might*."

Broch sucked in air, a tiny *whine* rounding out the end of his gasp. It was the sound a wee lassie might make, but he didn't have time to wonder how it had escaped *his* lips.

"Ye think?"

Pete finished his business. "What I have here, is a perfect penis."

"It is?"

Pete nodded. "Yup."

Broch looked at Pete and then himself and found few similarities.

"Och."

Pete adjusted his drawers. "You can get someone to fix it for you though."

"Howfur?"

"Get it cut down."

Broch gasped again and slapped his hand over his mouth, surprised by his squeal a second time.

Howfur ah keep makin' that noise?

"Cut it *aff*?" he asked.

Pete moved to the mirror and fixed his hair. "Yep."

Broch continued to gape, unable to wrap his mind around Pete's suggestion.

Pete leaned back to slap him on the arm. "Anyway, good talk, big guy."

Pete left the bathroom, whistling as if he didn't have a care in the world.

He didnae. He and his perfect penis.

Whistling. As if he'd told Broch to cut his hair, not his—

Broch stared down.

"Cut it *aff*?"

CHAPTER THREE

From her Jeep, Catriona stared at the closed door of Fiona's house, willing for it to *open* almost as much as she willed for it to stay *sealed*.

Forever.

She sighed and tapped her fingertips on her thigh, debating the pros and cons of hopping from the truck and pounding on Fiona's door. She deserved an explanation. The woman couldn't dump a ton of strange and upsetting information on her and then expect to skip to the safety of her home.

Catriona dropped her forehead to rest on the steering wheel.

Do I want to know what she meant?

If she listed everything that had happened to her in the last month, Catriona felt confident any sane person would agree she'd been through more than any normal human should have to bear in thirty days.

Of course, I'm not exactly normal. That's half the problem, isn't it?

Spotting a strapping Highlander's kilted butt on the set of Parasol Pictures' studio lot hadn't seemed like a big deal at the time. Her job as a "fixer" for the Hollywood studio had thrown her into a million odd scenarios—from fist-fighting aliens to coked-up children's icons.

Plaid-wrapped background talent wandering away from some in-production *Braveheart* knock-off should have been a cakewalk.

Instead, the background talent turned out to be an actual Highlander, thrown through time to her doorstep like the world's strangest Amazon package.

Brochan. No last name. Just Brochan-call-me-Broch-will-respond-to-*Kilty.*

Why had that giant man landed at Parasol? Couldn't he have spun through time and space and landed in New Jersey? Australia? Anywhere other than her lot?

Her adoptive father, Sean, served as the closest thing to a logical answer to that question.

Her borrowed dad was Broch's *real* dad.

Oh, and Sean had traveled through time, too. Decades earlier.

It made sense that Broch had somehow been drawn to be reunited with his father. That part of the story was so logical she'd nearly found a way to swallow everything else. *Why not?* What did she know? Maybe people came spinning through time every day and she was the last to know.

But right when she'd been ready to wrap her brain around Brochan's appearance, Sean dropped the bombshell that she, *herself*, might be from another time.

She had no memory of being in any other time. Maybe she'd been drinking white wine in whatever time she was from.

White wine was usually the culprit when she couldn't remember an evening.

She *did* have a very Scottish name. *Catriona.* Scottish spelling. And she'd arrived with the name. Sean didn't rename her after he'd found her as a child. Brochan claimed to remember her in his past, though it had taken him a while to put together that memory puzzle.

Maybe ancient Scotland sprang a leak.

She lifted her forehead from the steering wheel and rubbed at it, feeling the dimples of the faux leather pressed into her flesh like inverse braille.

Fantastic.

She glanced back at Fiona's door.

And then there's Fiona.

Catriona had hoped to never see Fiona again. The woman had a strange effect on Broch, and the witch had already tried to drug and seduce the Highlander once.

Catriona smoldered at the memory.

Then, out of nowhere, Fiona calls her for a *ride* from jail. Like Uber didn't even exist. Like they were *friends.*

Why did I pick her up?

Catriona sighed. She knew why. The woman was *mysterious.* Catriona thought she'd be smooth, draw Fiona into a conversation, tie her in verbal knots, make her admit she drugged Kilty...

Instead, Fiona hopped in the truck, smirky and confident, and told Catriona she was her *sister.*

Blech. Like this month couldn't get any worse.

A ringing pierced the silence and Catriona jumped, clutching at her heart.

For the love of—

She fumbled in her pocket and retrieved her phone to inspect the caller I.D.

Luther. Sean's best buddy and a fellow fixer for the studio. She answered, happy to be distracted from her thoughts.

"Hey, Luther. Nice timing. You just about stopped my heart."

Luther didn't bite and instead barreled into the reason for

his call like the efficient person he was. "Where's your father?"

"Sean's at the hospital with Broch. Broch caught a bullet from a crazy lady, but he'll be fine. Through and through near his armpit."

"His arm or his latissimus dorsi?"

"*Whatever*, you old gym rat. If he was built like me and didn't have those muscly wings under his pits the bullet would have missed him entirely, so you big beefy guys can suck it."

Luther chuckled. "You sound in a good mood."

"Oh, I'm just *giddy*."

"Well, we have a situation at the studio I was hoping you could look into."

Catriona rolled her eyes. All she wanted to do was go home and get some sleep. Maybe she'd get lucky and wake up in some new time, far, far away.

She paused.

Did she have to worry about that? Could she fly away to another time at any moment?

She sighed. She'd worry about that later.

Back to business.

"What's up?" she asked Luther.

"A woman is claiming Colin Layne knows where her missing sister is."

Catriona winced at the sound of Colin's name. She'd briefly dated the Parasol Pictures actor before he'd grown too famous for a peon such as herself. That was before she'd gotten smart enough to swear off actors entirely.

"Doesn't Sean usually deal with A-Lister problems?" she asked.

"I'm thinkin' this needs a woman's touch. The missing girl is Cari Clark—she works for us on and off. Bit parts. Her sister Violet's threatening to go to the police unless someone lets her question Colin."

"Think it's a ruse to meet Colin?"

Luther clicked his tongue. "Maybe. But I checked around and no one has seen Cari for a few days. She missed a fitting. And the sister doesn't sound like a nut."

"Okay. I'll talk to her. Got a number?"

"Got an address. Go and check things out. She wants Colin to go to her house for this meeting."

"Of course she does. She probably wants to show off to her neighbors. Hit me."

Luther rattled off an address in the Silver Lake neighborhood of Los Angeles.

"That's a pretty hoity-toity area for a rabid fan. Usually, these people don't have much going on in their own lives."

"She's got plenty of dough. She's a thoracic surgeon."

"Really?" Catriona considered asking if the *thoracic* was located anywhere near the *latissimus dorsi* but decided to let it go. "Okay. I'm on my way."

Catriona disconnected. With one last glare at Fiona's door, she shifted into gear and returned Sean's truck to the hospital.

Forget Fiona. I'm not falling for it.

She arrived back at the hospital and jogged to the waiting room to update Sean on the situation in Silver Lake.

Sean sat waiting for Broch in the same threadbare chair, reading an *actual* magazine with a perfectly good smartphone in his pocket.

He listened to her story and then weighed in. "Go ahead and take care of Cari Clark before whatever this is gets too far ahead of us. I'll wait for Broch."

She nodded. "See if you can get hold of Colin for me? Squeeze him for a little information?"

"Wouldn't *you* be better at that?" asked Sean with a wink.

Catriona glowered at him. "Don't *even*."

Sean chuckled. "Sorry. I'll give him a ring."

Spinning on her heel in an exaggerated snit for comic effect, Catriona left and drove to the address Luther had provided her.

Fans found infinite ways to finagle introductions to studio talent, but the persistent ones usually turned out to be teenagers, women with thirty cats, or guys who built doll versions of celebrities from mannequin parts purchased online. A female thoracic surgeon living in an expensive neighborhood didn't fit the mold.

Catriona parked in front of a well-appointed Spanish bungalow. Letting herself through the unlocked front gate, she entered a landscaped courtyard and knocked on a large, ornate front door so massive it made her knuckles hurt.

A middle-aged woman answered wearing a beige sweater set and khaki shorts, her hair hanging in smooth, neat ringlets that brushed the top of her shoulders. Around her throat hung a delicate gold cross and on her left ring finger balanced a large diamond.

Catriona grunted *huh* aloud without meaning to.

She doesn't look crazy at all.

She inhaled a surreptitious sniff.

House doesn't smell like cats.

"Is that lavender?" she asked aloud.

The woman's hand fluttered to her throat as she scanned Catriona from head to toe and back again. "My perfume, yes. Can I help you?"

"Are you Violet?"

"Who's asking?"

That's a yes.

"My name's Catriona Phoenix, I work with Parasol Pictures. They said you wanted to talk to someone?"

Violet frowned. "I wanted to talk to Colin Layne."

"Yes. We take your concerns seriously. But you have to

understand not everyone requesting an audience with our actors has legitimate needs. Can I talk to you first?"

With a sigh, the woman relented and took a step back. "Fine. Come in."

She turned to walk toward her living room and Catriona followed, closing the door behind her.

"I'm Dr. Violet Clark." The woman took a position in front of her sofa and offered a hand to shake. "Please. Have a seat."

Catriona sat and studied her hostess. A pretty, mocha-skinned woman of means, nothing about her or her professionally decorated home rang any warning bells. If anything, she seemed *too* perfect. That didn't bode well for Colin. Maybe he *had* done something wrong. Cari had probably run off to nurse an aching heart.

"Would you like some coffee?" asked Violet.

"No. I don't want to take up more of your time than I need to."

Plus, I should probably get back to the hospital where a recently shot Highlander is waiting for me.

"So, why do you want to talk to Colin?"

Violet took a deep breath. "He's dating my younger sister, Cari, and she's gone missing."

"How long since you last heard from her?"

"About a week."

"That isn't very long—"

The woman shook her head as if the motion could render Catriona's words silent. "We talk on the phone *every day*. She'd never disappear like this without letting me know."

"Could you have missed a message? Or—"

"No. I've thought of everything. Her roommate says she hasn't been home for over a week. I was about to go to the police when I thought Colin—since he's famous—had taken her somewhere where *he* couldn't be found, for privacy. Is that possible?"

"Very possible," said Catriona, though she suspected it wasn't. Colin was in the middle of a shoot, not tucked in a Parisian love nest, avoiding paparazzi.

"Tell you what. Give me a day to talk to Colin and let me see if I can find your sister?"

The tension in Violet's shoulders released. "Thank you. Thank you so much. I can't tell you how much I appreciate this. I'm so worried."

"I'm sure she's fine. We'll get it worked out." Catriona stood to leave. "Do you have a picture of your sister I could borrow?" She wanted to search the house for shrines dedicated to Colin Layne, but suspected that request wouldn't go over as well.

Violet moved to a dark wood hutch and retrieved a photo from the drawer. "She had these done back when she first started trying to get famous herself."

Violet handed Catriona a professional headshot of a smiling, younger version of herself.

"She looks a lot like you."

Violet nodded. "We have two sisters in between who look like each other. Cari and I have always had a bond. We favor our mother."

Catriona felt her cheek twitch. That's what Fiona had said about her—that she favored her mother. Fiona was apparently a daddy's girl.

Catriona took the photo.

"Thank you. We'll get a hold of Colin and get right back to you."

Catriona turned to leave, but Violet's sad expression gave her pause. She took the woman's hand in her own.

"I want you to know we take this very seriously. I *will* find out if Colin has any knowledge that could help you find Cari."

Violet patted her hand.

"Thank you. I appreciate it."

Catriona said her goodbyes. As she walked through the courtyard, she glanced back to find Violet watching her with that same sad look. Feeling the urge to offer more hope, she called back. "I'll find her. I promise."

Violet smiled.

Catriona immediately regretted her statement.

I know better than to make promises.

But, Cari was findable. Colin was a self-centered heel. Cari was probably somewhere crying on a girlfriend's shoulder.

She made her way back to her Jeep and called Sean.

"Hey, did you get hold of Colin?" she asked at the sound of his answer.

"Yes. He said he didn't know anything but he'd be happy to talk to us tomorrow at the studio. Ten o'clock, his trailer."

"You or me?"

"You, if you don't mind."

"*Why*?" The word sounded a little whinier than she meant it to sound.

"I'm on my way back to my house right now with Broch."

"Is he okay?"

"Yes. He's fine. Just needs some rest."

Catriona fell silent, mulling the pros and cons of driving to Sean's herself. He lived far from the studio, but she couldn't wait to talk to him about what Fiona had told her, and she wanted it to be somewhere she could read his expressions. She wasn't entirely sure he was always honest with her when it came to their time-traveling past.

"I think I'm going to come out to your house too if you don't mind."

"No problem. Plenty of room for everyone—as long as you get your butt back to the studio tomorrow by ten. Something up?"

"No. I mean, I'm not sure, to be honest. Fiona had a lot to

share."

"Like what?"

She sighed.

"I'll talk to you about it when I get there."

"Okay. See you then."

Catriona disconnected and dropped her phone into the Jeep's cup holder. She pulled from the curb and headed for Sean's, wishing very much the old man didn't love living in the middle of the desert.

CHAPTER FOUR

One Week Ago

Cassidy hung in the shadows of the apartment building watching the corner where the girl would appear. She'd removed her spurs to keep from janglin' because Cassidy *always* had spurs that jingle-jangled-jingled like Santa's sleigh bells.

She kicked up a heel to show everyone, but there were no spurs. No jangling. There was no audience, either.

This time she'd have a private audience.

One girl.

What was her name?

Right. *Cari.*

What a stupid name.

She didn't even spell it right. It looked as if someone started writing a name and then gave up.

Pay attention. You'll only get one chance to do this right.

Cari would park her car and lock it. The beep would be loud enough to hear.

Then like when ol' Cookie rang the dinner bell, Cassidy would come a runnin'.

Bee-Beep!

There it was.

Cassidy crouched lower behind the trashcans, the ruffles of her skirt brushing the tops of her boots.

Cari Clark walked down the side alley toward her door, fiddling with her keys as she searched for the one to open her apartment. Cari smiled as if she'd had a good night.

Fury exploded in Cassidy's chest. She clenched her fists to keep from lunging forward too soon.

We'll see how good a night it is, partner.

Cari stopped in front of her steps. She'd noticed the doll, sitting on the corner of the stoop, farthest from the stairs.

The bridge of her nose wrinkled.

Cassidy leaned forward.

Take it.

Cari hung her purse on her arm and walked around the stairs to pluck the doll from its perch. She turned it over and back again, studying the cowgirl outfit. The hair sprung from either side in braided pigtails. On the back of the doll's little vest, it said, *Cassidy Cowgirl,* written in pen.

Cassidy didn't know how to sew well enough to stitch the lettering, so she'd penned it. She was much better at ropin' and ridin' than sewin'.

That's for darn tootin'.

Cassidy watched Cari as she turned the doll over in her hands.

The moment is passing. Do something.

Cari fumbled the doll and it dropped to the ground. She laughed at her clumsiness, sounding a little drunk.

She bent over to retrieve the toy.

Cassidy jumped to her feet and lifted her miner's pickaxe high in the air. As she did, the tip of her boot bumped the trashcan.

Cari gasped and straightened at the sound.

Both women froze, gazes locked in the glow cast by Cari's front door light. Cassidy saw confusion clouding Cari's eyes. Flooding them. Momentarily blinding her to the threat.

The pickaxe arced through the air and embedded in Cari's skull.

Her eyes shut.

As Cari crumpled to the ground, the pick stuck in the bone, pulling Cassidy forward. The rattle sound of tumbling plastic trashcans echoed through the night as both women collapsed in a heap, one on top of the other.

Cassidy lifted herself from the ground and jerked on the pickaxe. It remained stuck. She found a better angle and tried again. The pickaxe popped free. Blood and brain matter spilled from the wound.

Cassidy dropped the ax and fumbled for the can of expanding sealant tucked in the inside pocket of her leather vest. From another pocket, she pulled a crumpled pink paper and poked it into the hole in Cari's skull with the tip of the sealant's straw.

Read that. Think about what you did.

The sealant came next, pumping into the gap.

The leaking stopped.

Cassidy dragged Cari's body to the bottom of the stairs and galloped to the hose hanging on the side of the building to spray away any remnant of the mess.

She retrieved the large sack tucked into the waistband of her skirt. Unfolded, it fit neatly over Cari's body.

Head 'em up, move 'em out.

She grabbed the girl's purse and threw it into the sack with her, before dragging the body down the alley to her car.

Time to set the trap.

Yee-ha!

CHAPTER FIVE

Broch watched Pete leave the men's room. He allowed his uplifted gown to drop and cover him before exiting himself, wandering back toward the room where the doctor had stitched his gunshot wound.

The doctor looked up from his computer. "Ah, there you are Mr., uh..."

"Broch."

"Right. Mr. Broch. You're all good to go."

Broch nodded.

The doctor stood and Broch stared at his extended hand, mulling over the conversation he'd had with Pete in the bathroom.

Shuid ah ask him aboot nipping aff mah—

The doctor's hand bobbed ever so slightly, reminding him of its presence.

Broch shook it.

No. Ah cannae say it.

The doctor gathered up his things. "You can put your clothes back on. Be careful not to strain those stitches and..."

The doctor picked up the empty pill bottle sitting on the counter and scowled.

"Didn't we fill this prescription for you?"

Broch blinked at the man. He wasn't sure what *prescription* was. Usually, he could piece together the meaning of modern words from context, but at that moment, the man might as well have been speaking Greek.

"Na?" he guessed.

The doctor's frown intensified. "Hm. I'll have them waiting for you downstairs when you check out. I'm not sure why they would bring us the bottle and not the pills."

The doctor left the room and Broch eased back into his clothes, staring forlornly at his manhood as he tucked it into his fancy new underwear.

It was like staring at a friend who'd betrayed him.

He shuffled down the hall and rode the elevator to the waiting area, head hanging, replaying Pete's words over and over in his head.

Sean glanced over as he entered the waiting room and perked at the sight of him.

Och. There was his answer.

Mah Da. He wid ken.

"Ready to go?" asked Sean.

"Aye."

Sean frowned. "Are you okay? Are you in pain?"

If ye only knew.

Broch couldn't find the words to tell the man what weighed on his mind.

"Where's Catriona?" he asked instead.

Sean hooked a thumb toward the door. "She had to run out. I'll take you to my house to recuperate unless you'd rather go to your apartment?"

Broch sighed. His apartment sat beside Catriona's. He couldn't be together with her now. Not until—

He looked at Sean and his father put a hand on his good shoulder.

"What is it, boy?"

Broch gasped a mighty breath. "Ah don't wantae cut aff mah wee man."

The words tumbled from his lips before he could stop them.

Heads in the waiting room turned.

Sean froze, his jaw falling slack.

"Uh, how 'bout we talk about this in the car..."

His father looped an arm around his and walked him from the hospital to his truck. Broch was glad to see Sean had brought the truck. His other car—the *Jag*, as Sean called it— was too small.

Sean motioned to the passenger side door. "Get in."

Broch did as he was told. He put an elbow on the armrest and sat with his chin in his palm, staring out the window, bouncing his bottom lip against his upper.

Mah face feels funny.

Sean hopped into the driver's side and remained silent until they were on the road.

"What was *that*?" he asked as he pulled onto the highway.

As Broch turned to look at him, his neck collapsed like a noodle, failing to support the weight of his skull. His head swung to the left and bounced off the headrest before he found a way to balance his skull once more. He steadied as Sean glanced at him, eyebrow cocked.

"Whit?" asked Broch. He'd forogotten what they'd been talking about.

"What was that you screamed back in the hospital. Something about cutting off your wee—?" Sean snorted a laugh and shook his head. "I think I misheard you."

Broch frowned, remembering, and took a deep breath.

"He said ah need tae cut it aff," he said.
"Cut *what* off?"

"My—" Broch gripped his crotch.

Sean scowled.

"Your *doctor* told you that? But you were shot in the arm—"

"Na. Nae mah doctor. *Pete*. Catriona's friend."

"No-see-um? The studio's doctor?"

"Aye."

"You saw Pete in the hospital, and he said you have to cut off your...*thing*?"

"Aye."

"Were you shot there too?"

"Na."

Broch's head swung the other way and thunked against the side window. The cars outside *whooshed* by and he watched them go, the steady rhythm like the sound of the sea...

He made the noise with his rubbery lips. "*Whoosh. Whoosh.*"

"*Broch.*"

Broch snapped from his traffic-induced trance.

"Whit?"

"Can you hear me?"

"Aye."

"You phased out there for a moment. Now tell me exactly what Pete said."

"He said ah had tae cut it off."

"Why?"

"He said 'twas tae big. That it wid frighten Catriona—"

Sean exploded with laughter.

Broch scowled. "It's nae funny."

Sean covered his mouth as if he needed to physically stop his mirth. "Broch—first off, Pete's an *ass*. He was kidding with you."

"He wis?"

"Of course he was."

"Bit his keeked different—"

"The man is a hundred and forty pounds soaking wet. I would imagine it *is* different. Might be half the reason he mentioned it."

"Bit he said Catriona wid be terrified—"

Sean shook his head. "Look, I don't want to drag Catriona into this. But I'm telling you, I'm sure you don't have anything to worry about."

"So ah dinnae hae tae cut it aff?"

"Absolutely not."

Broch inhaled a great gulp of air and released.

"*Pete*," he said at the end of his exhale. "Pound Pete."

He liked the way the P noise felt.

His head lolled until his chin rested on his chest, his lips hanging from his face like two slabs of beef. He began to make a *puh puh* sound, enjoying the popping noise they made.

He tilted his head, chin still pressed down and spotted Sean squinting at him.

Broch squinted back. "Problem?" he asked with the same popping P.

"I'm thinking you might have bigger problems than Pete."

"Pete said 'twas a big *problem* if ye ken whit ah mean." Broch barked one loud laugh at his joke, devolving into giggles he found difficult to control.

"Broch, pay attention."

Broch pressed his lips together to stop laughing. At least he thought he did. They were too numb to know for sure. "Hmmm?"

"Did you take any pills? Your pupils are like pinholes."

"Pinholes. *Pin*holes. Pin*holes*." Broch repeated the word several more times. It never sounded quite right to his ear.

"*Broch*. Did you take any pills?"

"Aye. *Pin*holes. The doctor gave them tae me." He fished in his pockets and produced the empty pill bottle, holding it aloft like a trophy. "They're brilliant. Pinholes. *Pinholes.* Pills. Pills *Pills.* Pah..*Paaaaaaaaaah..*"

"Is that bottle *empty*?"

Broch shook the bottle. Silence reigned.

"Aye."

"How many were in there?"

He shrugged. "Four. Same as the first time."

"The *first* time?"

Sean pulled off to the side of the road and snatched the bottle from Broch's hand. "He gave you *two* bottles of these?"

"Aye." Broch poked at his face. It felt a little like his lips were sliding off and he wanted to make sure they'd stay put.

Sean read the label and his shoulder slumped. "You're lucky, these aren't a high dosage, but you still shouldn't have taken *eight* of them."

Broch held up an indeterminate amount of fingers. "*Nine.* He gave me one tae start."

Sean pointed to the door. "Get out."

"Whit?"

"Get out of the truck and make yourself throw up."

"Whit?" Broch started to laugh. He wasn't sure why. Sean looked *angry*. It was hilarious.

Sean hopped out to walk around the truck and open Broch's door. He pulled the Highlander from the cab. Broch stumbled and caught himself on the door.

"Och, yer manhandlin' me—"

Sean pointed at the ground. "Throw up."

"Howfur?"

"Put your fingers down your throat. You have to throw up those pills or you could overdose and die."

Broch scowled. Dying didn't seem like a good idea. Passed away. *Passed. Pound Pete until he's passed. Puh puh...*

He stumbled away from Sean to lean against a great metal railing and tickle the back of his throat with his middle and index fingers. It only took a moment before the meager contents of his stomach hit the pavement.

Sean looked at the mess.

"Good. Four of them were barely dissolved. Get back in the truck."

Broch clambered into the cabin and Sean shut his door before returning to the opposite side to take his place in the driver's seat.

Sean pulled back onto the highway and Broch shut his eyes. His brain wobbled in his skull, demanding sleep.

"Ah willnae chop aff mah wee man," he mumbled.

Sean patted his knee. "No chopping."

Sean's phone rang and he answered. Broch could tell it was Catriona on the opposite end of the line.

He smiled.

CHAPTER SIX

Catriona tossed her purse onto Sean's kitchen table with the clattering of carelessly stowed sunglasses scratching against loose change and lipstick. She spotted the top of Sean's head through the kitchen window and leaned across the sink to get a better view.

Sean sat on his patio with whiskey in hand. No sign of Brochan in sight.

She took a deep breath. Quiet time with Sean had become a minefield since Broch showed up and their family's time-traveling history began to spill. The last time they talked, Sean told her, as a little girl, she sometimes popped from one room to another.

Why he didn't have me exorcised by a priest, I don't know.

She had no *popping powers* as an adult. That was a good thing. She could think of a few times she might have made a real ass of herself if given the chance. Popping into a cheating boyfriend's apartment unannounced, for example.

Her photographic memory proved to be the only remnant of those unique abilities. Sean suggested her mind could pop back and revisit a memory any time she needed it. Sort of quasi-time travel, where only her memory flew back for a refresher.

Which she had to admit was pretty cool.

She opened the sliding door to join Sean.

Here we go.

"How's the big guy?" she asked, taking a seat on the opposite side of the patio table.

Sean smirked and shook his head. "It's been quite a day."

"What happened?"

"Well, it seems our friend Dr. Pete told Broch his man-parts were too big and he needed to cut it off so it would look more like his."

Catriona, who'd been allowing the sparkling turquoise blue of Sean's pool to hypnotize her away from her day, felt her attention yanking back to the present. She turned away from the dancing glow of the underwater light with a snort of laughter.

"Please tell me you're kidding."

"Nope. Pete told him his member would terrify *you*, specifically. Not that I wanted to hear about any of that."

Catriona slapped her hand to her chest. "*Me?* How did I enter that inane conversation?"

Sean smirked. "I would imagine because Pete fancies you. He wanted to hobble the competition with insecurities."

"Psht." Catriona rolled her eyes. "Pete isn't after me. We've even talked about our mutual lack of interest."

"I suspect one of you was lying. But the important part is Broch—who was hopped up on *nine* pain pills at the time because no one's ever explained to him the concept of overdosing—had a meltdown in the waiting room, wailing he didn't want to cut off his willy."

Catriona covered her face with her hand, cackling.

"Please dinnae cut aff mah pee pee," she aped.

Sean laughed. "I think a couple of the gentlemen in the waiting room got up and left. The rest crossed their legs."

Catriona's waning laughter whipped into round two. She wiped away tears. "Stop. I can't take it." She took a deep breath. "Ooh...oh boy. Okay. He's good now?"

Sean nodded. "He's sleeping. I made him throw up at least four of the pills and the dosage wasn't high."

"Did you make him an appointment with a rabbi for his adult extreme-makeover bris?"

"I'll do that first thing in the morning."

Catriona giggled again and stood. "I need a drink."

Sean pushed the bottle toward her. She ducked inside to grab a glass and returned to pour herself a healthy shot.

"I have some news to share as well, but it isn't half as funny," she said, taking a sip. The tension in her shoulders began to ease.

"What's that?"

"I left the hospital because Fiona texted me to pick her up from jail."

Sean cocked his head. "A woman you barely know, who drugged Broch before he had the chance to drug himself, texted *you*?"

"Yep."

"When did you give her your number?"

"Never. But remember, she was with a semi-conscious Broch for an evening. She could have easily gone through his phone."

"Good point. What did she want?"

"Well, that's the funny part. I think she really did want a ride home, but then she dropped a bomb—she implied *she's* a time-bender herself—and, oh—that she's my sister and our father is looking for us."

Sean's expression fell slack. "What?"

Catriona nodded. "That was my reaction, more or less. She said she and I being in the same place would make it easier for him to find us. And from her tone, I'm guessing that's not a good thing for anyone."

Sean sat back. "Like he's drawn to you both somehow?"

"I was hoping you'd know. Is that a thing with you people? I mean, *us* people?"

"If it is, it's above my pay grade. Though, I've often wondered the chicken-and-the-egg thing with Broch being here."

"What do you mean?"

"Was I sent to this place because Broch was destined to show up years later? Or was he sent here because I'm here?"

Catriona grimaced. "I don't think you have enough whiskey for us to get into that one tonight."

"Probably not. What else did Fiona say?"

Catriona shrugged. "Nothing. She walked into her house and shut the door."

"You didn't follow her?"

Catriona chuckled. "When men go crashing through people's doors to get answers, they look like tough guys. When women do it, we look like lunatics. Either way, we all end up in jail. I wasn't going to give her an excuse to call the cops on me. For all I know, that was half the game."

Sean nodded slowly. "Very wise. Women should probably be in charge of the world."

"*Duh.*"

They sat staring at the pool in silence for several minutes. Catriona was grateful for the peace. It had been a tough day.

When he finished his glass, Sean stood. "I'm going to retire. I assume you're staying?"

She nodded. "Tomorrow I'll go back to town and do a little digging into Fiona Duffy. She's never been more than a blip on my radar. Maybe she deserves a little more scrutiny."

"Maybe she deserves a good kick in the lady balls."

Sean kissed the top of her skull. "Don't stay up too late worrying about crap."

He opened the slider and Catriona reached out to touch his wrist.

"Hey. You'd tell me if you knew anything more about my history, wouldn't you? Is there anything else about any of us I need to know?"

He patted her fingers with his opposite hand.

"No. I'd tell you if I knew."

She stared at him, trying to read his inscrutable expression.

Hopeless. Nothing to do but believe him.

With a final smile, he disappeared inside the house.

Catriona remained seated for the rest of her drink. It felt as though the turquoise pool water, sparkling beneath the desert moon, should inspire epiphanies about fate and time, mysteries and love. Instead, all it did was make her sleepy.

Or maybe that was the whiskey.

She pushed her glass into the center of the table and stood, reaching to the sky to stretch her back. She wasn't of the mind to solve mysteries tonight. For all she knew, Fiona was a nut. She'd been a suspect in a kidnapping and she'd date-drugged Broch. The bitch had been floating around Hollywood as a B-list actress and tabloid temptress for some time. She didn't work for Parasol, so they'd never had a reason to meet until Fiona's recent nefarious involvement in their last job. In Catriona's opinion, Fiona had gotten off easy with a couple of days in jail.

Catriona's gaze drifted to the stars visible in the un-light-polluted desert sky. She did her best to let it all go... stress... confusion... suspicions...

She wandered inside, weaving through the kitchen and into the hallway without the need to turn on a light. She'd grown up in the little house with Sean and could walk the rooms blindfolded.

Heading down the hall she passed the guestroom,

pausing to peek inside.

Broch lay on his stomach, sound asleep beneath a thin layer of covers. She watched the steady rise and fall of his back.

What do you know, you big slab of Scottish haggis?

Did *he* know more than he'd shared with her? Was he up to something?

She chewed on her lip, considering.

He did take a bullet for me...

But that was the oldest trick in the book, wasn't it? Take a bullet for someone so they'll believe anything you say?

Maybe not. Seemed like a pretty extreme way to gain someone's confidence.

With a grunt, Catriona headed for her bedroom

I'm watching you, Highlander.

CHAPTER SEVEN

Edinburgh, Scotland. 1833.

Broch stared at the ceiling of his adoptive father's blacksmith forge.

It had been a year since they buried Catriona. He'd been holding her in his arms when her father shot her. Broch suspected her father had been aiming for *him*, but he'd never had the chance to find out. The man had disappeared. Broch guessed he'd left Scotland and returned to America, abandoning the body of his daughter for fear he'd be dragged to jail and hanged.

With no one to tend to the girl, Broch claimed the body, though he'd only known her for a week.

The time didn't matter. He'd loved her. Of that he was certain.

Broch had never buried anyone before. His friend, Gavin, had talked to his rich father and the old man offered Broch a lair on the family land. They had a small service with candles and a fine meal, where Broch pushed beef around his plate until it was time to go.

Nearly a year ago.

Things never felt the same.

How many nights had he watched the light from the fire dance on his ceiling, feeling as though his chest would crack clean open? Anchored by sadness, any dreams of travel had died with Catriona. Any joy he'd found pounding metal for his father had dissipated. Gone was the thrill of completing a sword behind his father's back. The news that he'd graduated from apprentice to blacksmith had barely raised his pulse. The old man was in ill health and had bestowed his responsibilities upon his boy. Now each day Broch performed by rote.

What was the point of anything without Catriona?

Something rustled in the corner of the shop and Broch rolled over, certain he'd find a rodent creeping toward his hay-stuffed kip. Enough of the local folk paid his father with meat and milk so they didn't need to keep animals themselves. Broch felt grateful to not have to share his bed with livestock. He had friends much less well-to-do than Gavin who lived in croft houses with their families *and* their animals, all of them stuffed in the same windowless box.

Broch's eye traced the curve of a shadow standing in the corner of the room.

It was no rat.

His eye adjusted to the dying light of the fire. He watched as a fair-faced young man appeared from the darkness as if rising from a darkened loch.

"Who are ye?" asked Broch.

The man raised a knife and whispered. "Stay in your bed."

Broch's eyebrows hoisted like the sails of a ship. "Ye're American?"

"Just stay there." The figure inched toward the door, still brandishing the knife in his direction.

Broch stood.

"I said stay *there*!" hissed the trespasser.

"Ye sound lik' someone ah ken."

Broch lunged forward and the figure did the same, blade slashing. Broch dodged the point and caught the wrist of the hand holding the weapon, pushing it and his midnight visitor against the wall with a clattering of pots and tools.

"Brochan?" called the old blacksmith from his bedroom in the back of the shop.

Broch pressed his body against the intruder's, certain that his guess had been correct.

It was no fair-faced young man robbing his blacksmith shop.

It was a *woman*.

"Be quiet," he whispered in her ear. "Ah willnae harm ye."

He called to the back of the shop. "Sorry Da, ah wis up takin' a pish."

"Och. Mind yerself." The old man grunted.

Brochan returned his focus to the butterfly he'd pinned to his wall. The whites of her wild eyes glowed in the dark.

Leaning hard against her to keep her still, he twisted the knife from her hand and pulled at her wrist, dragging her through the door and into the outdoor workshop area.

The moment they stepped into the cool evening the girl twisted, desperate to break free.

"You're *hurting* me," she whined.

"Hold, 'n' it wilnae hurt."

"What do you want?"

"Whit dae *ah* want? Ye were in *mah* home."

The girl sniffed, copping what he felt a haughty air for a common criminal.

"I'm hungry. I was looking for food."

"Thare's a tavern doon thare. Ye hae na coin?"

"No, I *hay nah coin*. Why would I creep around your sad little hovel if I had money?"

Broch scowled. "Ye'd dae weel nae tae mock the fowk who's land yer in, *American*."

It was darker outside than it had been in the house, but he thought he saw the young woman roll her eyes. Her fire reminded him of Catriona.

"Are all wummin fae America as saucy as ye?" he wondered aloud.

She smiled. "There are no women in America like *me*."

"Ah hae an argument wi' ye oan that point." Brochan released her wrist and she rubbed it with her opposite hand but did not run. He motioned for her to leave.

"Git oot."

She remained rooted in her spot, so close to him he could hear her breathing.

"I still haven't solved my problem. I need food."

Brochan found it difficult not to laugh. "Och, whit ahm ah thinkin'? Where are mah manners. Shuid ah tak' ye inside and cook ye a meal?"

"You could take me to the tavern, but first you should put on some britches."

Broch glanced down and realized he'd leapt from his kip stark naked to trap the intruder.

He found himself amused by his oversight. He had to admit, this evening was the first he'd felt some semblance of his old self.

"Aye. I kin dae that."

He opened the door and strode back inside to grab his kilt and a shirt. Glancing over his shoulder to be sure the thieving woman wasn't peeking in his door, he lifted a pot sitting on another and pulled some coins from inside the second. He slipped the money into his leather sporran and returned outdoors.

"Och, yer still here," he said, pretending to be disappointed.

The woman leaned against his workbench, her arms crossed against her chest as if she were annoyed he'd made her wait. He'd expected her to run, but on second thought, supposed the bandit didn't have a reason to flee since he'd agreed to buy her supper.

How she'd transformed from a robber to a dinner date, he wasn't sure.

Without pause, he strode toward the tavern.

"Follow me."

She scurried up beside him.

"So you've met American girls before?" she asked.

He sighed. "Aye. Seems the town is choked wi' thaim lately."

He reached the door of the Sheep Heid Inn and jerked it open to enter. Only the bartender and two men playing cards in the corner remained from the early evening rush.

A man sat behind the bar, his eyes closed, his head resting on his hand. The lamp's light dipped into the pocked surface of his bald skull.

"Kin we git somethin' tae eat, John?" Brochan asked. John always appeared asleep, but rarely was.

True to form, the man shook his head without opening his eyes. "Cook's lang gaen."

Broch turned and stared into the haunted eyes of the woman behind him. Though her dark hair had been chopped nearly as short as a boy's, and hunger had replaced the feminine curve of her face with sharp angles, in the brighter light of the tavern, there was no mistaking his intruder for a boy. She filled her shirt in ways no boy ever could.

As he studied the lines of her face, he felt the tendrils of a creeping realization.

She looks lik' Catriona.

There was no mistaking it. The full lips, the stormy green eyes, pale complexion and dark hair—there were differences, certainly, but—

The girl put her hands on her hips and stared back at him.

"Are you going to stand there staring at me, or are you going to buy me some food?"

He sighed.

At the sound of the woman's voice, John's eyes opened and he straightened in his seat. Broch looked at him, silently begging for a favor.

John yawned. "Tell ye whit. If ye promise nae tae stay lang, ah will pat together some meat and bread fur ye. Then ahm needin' tae close up."

John's eyes had locked on the girl. No doubt, he, too, had been struck by her tragic beauty and been inspired to feed her.

Broch nodded. "Aye. Thank ye. We willnae be lang."

"Ale as well?"

"Aye. Twa."

Broch moved to a table on the opposite side of the bar from the card players. The men watched them with steady interest. Broch held the stare of one to be sure the patron understood he wanted no interference. With a sniff, the man returned his attention to his hand.

Broch sat and the girl took a place across from him.

"Sae, who are ye?" he asked.

She tossed her hair from her eyes. "Fiona."

Broch struggled to keep his composure. Fiona had been the name he'd known Catriona by until the last moments of her life. Her father had dubbed her so, though he didn't understand why.

"Ahm Brochan."

"Nice to meet you." Her eyes darted back to the bar, searching for any sign of the man arriving with food.

Brochan tapped her finger with his own to recall her attention.

"How come yer rootin' through mah hame?"

"I told you. I was looking for food."

John appeared and dropped a plate of fatty meat and

bread before them. No sooner had the platter left his fingertips than Fiona grabbed a chunk and shoved it into her mouth.

Broch pushed the plate toward her. She glanced at him but didn't slow her chewing.

John left and returned to place two mugs of ale in front of them. Broch slid a coin toward him with a nod of thanks.

John returned to his post.

Broch took a swallow of his brew and watched the girl eat.

Whit wis it aboot Americans?

His love, Catriona, had been mistreated by her cruel father. Now it seemed he'd found another American left in the cold by someone.

Fiona put the last hunk of bread in her mouth and gulped at her ale. She looked up at him, breathing more as if she'd run a race than raced through a meal.

"Howfur does an American lassie lik' ye end up 'ere alone?" he asked.

She licked at the corner of her mouth and grinned.

"Who says I'm alone?"

CHAPTER EIGHT

Present Day

"Rise and shine, big boy," said Catriona, slapping the back of Kilty's exposed calf muscle. It didn't appear he'd moved the entire evening.

Groaning, the Highlander lifted his head, a string of spit linking him to the pillow like a leash.

"Och, mah heid. Ah'm feelin' sae groggy."

Catriona crossed her arms against her chest. "Pain meds will do that to you."

He rolled over and struggled to sit up, wincing as the movement pulled at the bandages beneath his arm.

"Pain meds?" he said in the strange, exaggerated American accent he used when saying words or phrases new to his vocabulary.

"Those pills you took at the hospital that Sean made you throw up."

"Th' wee bitter candies."

Catriona clucked the side of her mouth. "Yes, see, that's the problem. They aren't *candies*. They're *medication*. Imagine a kind of mushroom that heals the plague or *dragon-lung* or whatever you people got back then. Now imagine that mushroom is *poison* if you take too much of it. The same herb that could have saved you, kills you instead."

"Mushrooms arenae an herb."

Catriona threw him his t-shirt. "The genius who ate Percocets like M&Ms is going to make fun of *me*?"

He stood and slipped his tee over his head, easing his sore arm through the hole. "Sae yer sayin' that colorful wee pill is a poisonous mushroom?"

"For all intents and purposes."

Sean appeared in the doorway. "How are you feeling, Broch?"

Broch rubbed at his hair. "Mah heid's feelin' a bit cloudy if ye mist ken."

"How about your wound?"

"Sore."

"That's why they gave you a bottle of pills. If you space them out, they're safe and offer steady pain relief."

Broch frowned. "Bit ah ate them all."

"I have some here. I'll lend you a few to take back to the lot with you. Just follow the instructions this time."

"Ah will. Thank ye."

Sean left to fetch the pills. Catriona caught Broch adjusting the fit of his jeans and giggled.

"Sean told me what Pete said to you."

Broch's head swiveled. "He did?"

She nodded. "Pete was *teasing* you. You don't have Frankendick."

"Whit?"

"I've seen it before, remember? You're ah...*good*."

Between finding Broch naked on the lot and his fascination with showers, she felt as though she'd seen him naked more times in the last few weeks than she'd seen herself that way.

A smile curled the side of Broch's lips. "That's true. Ah hadn't thought o' that. Ye *hae* seen me in all mah glory. Ye didnae scream."

"No. And if yours doesn't look like Pete's, I dare say that's a good thing."

Broch scowled. "Ah'm aff tae kill that wee man neist time ah see him."

Catriona laughed and walked to the kitchen to find Sean slipping bread into a toaster that should have been outlawed in nineteen eighty-two. If his house ever burned down, she knew exactly where to point the fire investigators.

"You sure you don't want to stay for breakfast?" he asked at the sound of her footsteps on the creaky hallway floorboards.

"Nah. We'll pick something up on the way back to town. If I stay too long here in Shangri-La I'll never leave."

When Broch entered, Sean handed him half a glass of orange juice and pointed at a pill bottle on the table.

"Take one now and one around dinner. It will cut the pain. Keep it from throbbing."

Broch nodded and took a pill with his juice. They said their goodbyes and started the long drive back to the studio.

Halfway into the drive, Catriona caught Broch snorting himself awake, which explained his unusual silence. Normally when they drove somewhere, he'd spend the whole trip pointing out unfamiliar modern objects and asking, "Wit's that?" Those were the times she realized finding a Highlander was a little like adopting a five-year-old.

"Whit are we daein' taeday?" he asked, rubbing his face.

"I have a meeting at ten. You're not doing anything. You need to hold still and let that wound heal."

Broch groaned. "Ah cannae lay aroond in mah kip all day."

"Well, you're *going* to lay around in your kip all day."

She glanced at him to find him pouting, as he repeatedly stood up the zipper on his jeans and then flicked it back down. He was so fascinated with zippers that she felt guilty taking them for granted. If she'd been thrown into the future to find each morning people walked into a closet to shrink-wrap themselves instead of dressing, she imagined she'd be enthralled by the process the same way Broch was mesmerized by zippers.

She shuddered at the idea of shrink-wrapped clothing. The pressure to stay fit would be *terrible*.

"Last nicht ah dreamt aboot a lassie wi' mirk locks," said Broch, his voice nearly a mumble.

"Mirk?"

"Black. Her name wis Fiona."

Catriona turned her head so hard she nearly jerked the vehicle off the road. "What? Was it *her*? The real Fiona, not me?"

"Ah dinnae ken. It felt more lik' a memory than a dream, though."

"What do you remember?"

He scratched at his jaw. "She sneaked intae mah hoose tae rob it. She wis hungert, sae ah gave her some meat."

Catriona squinted. "Why does that sound like Highlander porn?"

"Whit?"

Catriona decided it was early in the morning to explain porn and ignored his question.

"You said Fiona broke into your house and you bought her dinner?"

"She wis hungert."

"Yeah, I got that. What else do you remember?"

He shrugged. "Nothing. Ye woke me."

Catriona pictured her last exchange with Fiona. The way the woman had smirked before walking saucily to her home, made her blood boil.

She thinks she knows everything.

Fiona hadn't mentioned Kilty during their conversation, but she *had* seemed fascinated with him. Maybe she remembered him, too? Maybe he was her brother...

No. Wait. If I'm her sister and he's her brother...

She glanced at Broch.

Oh no.

No. That's not possible. She and Broch couldn't be related because they already knew Broch was Sean's son, and Sean didn't have any long-lost daughters. He would have said something if he did. They didn't need a DNA test to prove that. Broch was a dead-ringer for a young Sean.

Whew.

But Fiona *did* seem obsessed with the Highlander. Maybe it was a sibling rivalry? Maybe Fiona wanted to steal little sis's boyfriend?

She glanced at Broch.

Is he my boyfriend now?

"Hey..." Catriona began her sentence slowly, unsure whether she wanted to hear the answer to her question. "You know how when you saw Fiona the first time, you thought she seemed familiar to you?"

"Aye. Ah tellt ye before ah hud her confused wit ye in mah dreams."

"Right, but what you just told me sounds like you *did* know the real Fiona."

Broch remained silent, staring at the dash.

Catriona started again. "There seems to be some sort of connection between you two—"

"Ye died." Broch spat the short sentence as if it had been building inside him for some time.

"What?"

"Ye *died*. In mah dream. We were in love bit ye died in

mah arms."

"I *died*?" She gaped. "You never told me *that*."

"Ah haven't hud the time, hae ah?" He motioned to his wound.

"I guess not."

Catriona fell silent but found it impossible to stay that way for long.

"How did I die? Consumption or something?"

"Ye were shot. Ah'm sure he wis trying tae shoot me, bit—"

"He? Who's *he*?"

"Yer faither."

Catriona felt the blood drain from her cheeks. Fiona said their father was searching for them—would probably find them now that they were together.

She guessed *together* meant *in the same year.*

At the time, being found by a father she'd never known didn't seem like such a horrible thing, but hearing that her old man had *shot* her in a previous life, thrust family reunions into a new light.

"You were there when my father shot me?"

"Aye."

"So what happened? Did I disappear and come to this time?"

Broch stared through the window, holding so still it looked as if someone had shut him down by flipping a switch in his back.

"Broch?"

He looked at her.

"Did I disappear?" she repeated. "After my father shot me?"

He shook his head. "Na."

She scowled. "What do you mean, *na*? That's what happened when Sean rescued me as a baby. He stabbed the bad

guy—who might have been my father, come to think of it—
and he sort of... *poof.*" She raised her hands far enough off the
steering wheel to simulate the dome of a tiny explosion.

"Na. Ah buried ye. Yer faither left yer body 'n' bolted. A
friend of mine gave me a lair tae lay ye doon."

"A lair?"

"A grave." He chuckled. "Ah lik' hae'n to explain things
tae *ye* once in a while." He held up his hands like claws and
continued in a scary voice. "It was a mirk, mirk, lair..."

"Very funny, but if we could get back to the part about me
being dead—you buried me? In Scotland?"

"Aye."

"So the bones of a *previous me* are laying in the Scottish
dirt somewhere right now?"

"Aye. Ah suppose."

She shivered.

How creepy.

She needed to remember exactly what Fiona had said.

Maybe I can work on that little memory trick of mine.

She closed her eyes for a moment and imagined sitting in
Sean's truck with Fiona. Her hand lying flat on her thigh. That
stupid smirk...

She could hear the woman's voice as if she were sitting
next to her now.

Who killed you? asked Fiona. *If you were born here, it means
you started from scratch. It means instead of jumping, body
intact, you left your body behind.*

That's it.

Fiona knew she'd been killed. It was the reason Catriona
had been a little girl, instead of arriving in this time as a full-
grown person the way Broch had.

What else had Fiona said?

...when he tried to kill me.

Their father had tried to kill *both* of them.

Catriona frowned.

Daddy is turning out to be a real jerk.

"...and then he started calling *me* Fiona," she said aloud.

"Whit?"

"While you were in the hospital, Fiona called me. She told me I'm her sister."

Broch turned to face her. "Yer *sister*? Why didnae ye tell me?"

"I just did. Like you said, it's been kind of a whirlwind here the last twenty-four hours."

He ran a hand through his hair. "Aye."

"But that explains why, in your earlier dreams, my father called me by *her* name."

"That's howcome ah wis muddled."

"But then you found out my real name."

"Aye. Ye tellt me right before ye were shot."

"And the real Fiona wasn't around?"

"Na."

Catriona sighed. She didn't like to put too much credence in dreams, but it seemed as though Broch's were his direct connection to his other life.

She touched his arm to get his attention. "Be careful of her. She's dangerous."

"In mah dream?"

"Yes. And in real life. Just be careful. I should get you a copy of *Nightmare on Elm Street*. Teach you how to fight people in your dreams, just in case."

He shook his head, his shaggy hair swinging. "Ah think they're memories. Ah cannae change them noo."

"Whatever. Just be careful."

Broch grunted and stared unblinking at the road.

Catriona couldn't tell whether he was deep in thought or the pain pills had kicked in.

CHAPTER NINE

Catriona pulled into the Parasol Pictures studio parking lot and, after snapping Broch awake, they walked to the front gate.

"Ah dinnae think ah lik' the pills," mumbled Broch, mid-yawn. "Thay mak' me sleepy."

Catriona called out to have the gate opened and slid a hand up and down Broch back to soothe him, careful to avoid his wound. "I imagine being shot takes a lot out of you, too. Don't blame it all on the pills."

He smiled and closed his eyes. "Nails."

Curling her fingers, she transformed her comforting rub into a proper back scratch and he writhed with pleasure.

She called for the gate again, and once more didn't hear the corresponding *click!* of the magnetic lock releasing. Peering into the guard box, she discovered it was empty.

Catriona put her hands on her hips. "That's not good."

She found the key on her ring that opened the walk-through portion of the elaborate, wrought iron front gate, but there was no excuse for the guard box to be unmanned. People tried to enter the studio all the time—both fans who needed to be turned away and VIPs who would need the gate opened to claim one of the coveted internal parking spots. She made a mental note to discover who *should* have been manning the box. If it was one of the old guards with whom she was friendly, she'd give them a warning. If it was someone new, she'd have to tell Luther. He was in charge of the day-to-day security and needed to know his employees were letting him down.

A few steps onto the studio screams caught Catriona's ear. Panicked shrieks on a Hollywood studio lot weren't strange. Actors were fake-murdered and fake-chased all the time. But something about *this* commotion didn't feel right. She pointed herself toward the noise and broke into a jog.

"You should go back to your apartment," she called over her shoulder, sensing Broch was on her heels.

He didn't answer. He usually ignored her when she said things he didn't want to hear.

Catriona ran down the side of the long stage building where they filmed *Ballroom Bounce,* a dancing competition show. Nearing the corner, she slowed to a stop and motioned for Broch to stay. She pointed to the wall to draw his attention there.

He was already staring at the spot. A bloody handprint smeared a foot and a half from its starting point, disappearing around the corner of the building.

She reached for her gun and found it missing.

Damn.

The police had taken her weapon before letting her on the ambulance to travel with Broch to the hospital the day before. She had another weapon in the Jeep and one tucked in her apartment, but neither would do her any good now.

The shouting began again, several voices together, some screaming, some barking orders. Catriona peeked around the blood-smeared corner and spotted a small crowd encircling a body on the ground. Judging by the high-heeled footwear, she guessed the supine body was female. This close to a dance competition show, though, heels and sparkly outfits didn't confirm sex one way or the other.

While the bulk of the crowd encircled the wounded woman, many had their attention on something beyond the scene. Catriona heard a man yelling at the top of his voice, something unintelligible.

Catriona strode from her hiding spot. The trail of blood that began on the studio wall continued on the ground in spatter leading to the body. As she neared the crowd, she spotted a crouching woman holding the hand of the dancer on the ground. A man in a skin-tight tuxedo squatted beside her, his hands on the dancer's throat.

The victim's eyes were open but dull as if someone had spun the dimmer switch in her head. Her skin was ashen. Her throat, and the man's hands pressing there, were covered in blood.

Catriona caught the man's eye. "What happened?"

"He tried to rip out her *throat*," yelped a woman behind her before he could answer.

"Who?"

The man in the tux adjusted the pressure on the dying woman's neck. "Timmy—he started tearing at her like an animal."

"I called 911. They're on the way," said another woman in the crowd. No sooner had the words left her lips than Catriona heard the sirens in the distance.

Catriona spotted a man in a guard uniform mingling with another smaller group farther down the lot. "That guard needs to get to the gate to let the ambulance in. Someone get him."

"I got it," said a man in yellow Spandex, sprinting away.

She turned her attention back to the tuxedoed young man. She didn't recognize him as a regular cast member and guessed he was a contestant. "Did you say *Timmy* did this?

Timmy Grey?"

A murmur of affirmation rose from the crowd.

Catriona shook her head, unable to wrap her brain around the information provided. Timmy Grey was a cartoonishly-foppish man of about one hundred and sixty pounds, fully dressed. If asked to make a list of people she thought capable of tearing out a woman's throat, dance judge Timmy Grey would sit near the bottom.

"Where is he?" she asked.

"They have him pinned over there." The man nodded his head to the right, his gaze never leaving the pool of blood creeping across the pavement beside him.

Catriona touched his shoulder. "You're doing great. Keep that pressure. They're almost here."

The man's jaw clenched and he nodded.

Catriona straightened and pushed her way through the onlookers to find Timmy Grey, the alleged attacker, huddled against the wall of another studio building, tearing at his skin, threads of blood running down his forearms. The crowd had trapped him there, encircling him and holding their arms wide like cowboys cornering a wandering calf.

Timmy's eyes were wild. He wore pressed-velvet cranberry-colored trousers and a shredded white shirt with a polka dot cravat still dangling from his throat by a thread.

Spotting her as she pushed through the crowd, Timmy turned to press his chest against the wall, clawing at the corrugated metal as if he thought he could climb to the roof like a cockroach and escape.

"Timmy!"

Timmy's head spun. His eyes locked on hers, his chest heaving.

Catriona raised her palms in an attempt to ease him. "Timmy. This isn't you—"

The dance judge pushed off the wall like a released

pinball and bolted toward her. The crowd loosed a collective yelp and stumbled back, desperate to avoid the blood-splattered maniac.

Timmy's fingers curled, clawing the space before him as if it were necessary to tear through the air to reach her. Though he was a diminutive man, years of dance training had made his body taut and his legs *fast*.

Too fast.

Unwilling to run and endanger the others, Catriona braced herself to catch her attacker, hoping when he hit she could steamroller him back and tackle him to the ground. The closer he grew, the more she doubted her plan. Three feet from her he opened his mouth so wide she thought his jaw might unhinge. He roared as if a demon sat at the helm of his body.

Timmy leaped, claws outstretched. Catriona was still calculating the best way to wrap Timmy tight without losing half her face, when an enormous fist buzzed past her shoulder and struck Timmy square in the nose, knocking him back and to the ground like a clattering board.

Heart still racing, Catriona couldn't help but flash a smile.
Kilty.

Broch pushed her behind him as Timmy sprang from the ground like a rising vampire. The little man lunged again, this time at Broch, who grabbed his child-sized wrists and twisted them behind his back. Timmy hissed like a feral cat, teeth snapping, his arms crisscrossed against his chest. Broch stood behind him, tying his arms like the bow of a gift package.

The wild dance judge kicked at Broch's shins until the Highlander knocked the back of Timmy's knees, folding him. They fell together, Broch on top, to the ground. Timmy's face hit first and Catriona watched a tooth bounce across the pavement to rest at her feet.

The crowd released a collective *"Ooooh...."*

Timmy continued to struggle until he fell limp beneath

Broch's weight.

"Are you sure he can breathe?" asked Catriona.

Broch tilted back his head to stare up at her, his brow covered in sweat.

"Does it maiter? The man's *mad*."

Blood spotted Broch's t-shirt in the vicinity of his wound. His bandage had to be soaked through, and Catriona feared the struggle had torn his stitches. She squatted beside him, checking to see if Timmy had been pressed into a pancake.

"Just ease up on him a little bit. I think you're crushing him."

Broch grunted, shifting his weight. "That wis the point." He shifted to his knees, pulling Timmy back and holding him like a shield in front of him. The small man's head hung like a broken chicken's neck, but he was breathing. His boney chest exposed where he'd shredded his shirt, Catriona counted his heartbeats at well over one hundred per minute. He had to have been knocked cold by his fall, or he'd still be raging. Something had his heart racing, even in his unconscious state.

She stood. Two ambulances arrived with several police vehicles in tow. She held her hand above her head, feeling responsible for the gawking crowd of Parasol dancers and employees.

"Everyone, please back up. We have to make way. You'll only be hindering our attempts to help these people. If you're injured, physically or mentally, please stand by that wall." She pointed to the wall of the dance studio as she shifted into *avoid litigation* mode, knowing there was little chance of success.

"He tore out her throat!" screamed someone on the verge of hysteria, but the crowd began to disperse. Those who didn't leave, backed to the outer edges of the scene.

No one stood against the wall. Catriona took some comfort there until her gaze began to sweep the scene.

There was blood *everywhere*.

Droplets, footprints, and smears stained the ground and walls. The EMTs fought to save the life of the girl. The man who had been applying pressure to her throat stood nearby, seemingly in shock, more blood than flesh visible on his hands.

Two officers ran toward Timmy and Broch, guns drawn but held low. Another pair approached the crowd, asking for them to remain calm and gather where the police could begin the interview process.

"The man who did this is there," said Catriona, pointing to Timmy as more galloping officers approached. "He's unconscious. The man holding him is my—" She wasn't sure what to call Broch. *Partner* sounded odd. She changed directions. "He works for me."

"Put him down," said a short, stocky officer, holstering his gun as he approached.

Broch lowered Timmy to the ground and stood as the officers untangled the unconscious man's arms and motioned to the EMTs to come forward.

"If he wakes up, be careful. He's definitely on something," warned Catriona.

One of the officers raised a hand. "We've got it from here."

Catriona took a step back and motioned for Broch to stand beside her. The EMTs rolled Timmy on his back, his mouth gaping, a dark gap yawning where his front tooth once sat. His lips and chin, scraped from his fall, had begun to swell.

Catriona hung her head and took a deep breath.

Some fixer I am.

This one had gotten away from her.

The girl would be lucky to live. Regardless of what had caused Timmy's frenzy, he wouldn't survive with his career intact.

He'd probably spend the rest of his life in jail.

Fixer   *fail.*

CHAPTER TEN

Luther arrived at the studio shortly after the ambulance doors shut on Timmy's victim. Catriona saw him dodge as the wailing vehicle tore toward Southern California Hospital. She waved to him and he broke into a trot, moving with agility uncommon in such a big man. Luther lumbered when he walked and jogged with the grace of a gazelle.

"What can I do?" he asked, eyeballing the blood-splattered Highlander at her side.

"We're going to be tied up with the police for a while. Broch brought down Timmy, so they're going to have questions for him."

Luther nodded to Broch. "Good job."

Broch nodded back using the tight-lipped, manly shorthand that apparently even men from other centuries understood.

Luther strained to catch a glimpse of Timmy, who lay restrained on the ground, his eyes now open and wide, staring at the sky, his chest heaving. The worst of his frenzy over, the dance judge seemed both agitated and dazed. The police pulled him to his feet and walked him toward the second ambulance.

"Did you get a chance to talk to Timmy?" asked Luther.

Catriona shook her head. "Not even close. He was out of his mind. It was all we could do to keep him from shredding his own arms."

"Drugs?"

"No doubt."

Luther pulled at his chin. "I'll take a peek in his dressing room. See if I can find anything."

Catriona nodded. Finding drugs before the cops was part of the job she didn't like, but mission number one was to *protect the studio's assets.* Not at *any* cost, but she lived in the grey area.

This time, *revealing* instead of *hiding* the drugs might be their best option. Drugs would be the only way to explain why Timmy had been insane.

Luther scanned the area. Catriona could see he was tracking potential witnesses—and potential lawsuits—as they wandered past.

"This is going to be a tough one," he said in his lowest baritone.

She nodded. "Agreed. The rest of the cast are being gathered in the *Ballroom Bounce* studio. I think they were filming packages for the upcoming show. At least we don't have to keep tabs on an entire studio audience."

Catriona spotted an officer headed in her direction and shooed Luther away before the authorities decided *he* needed to stick around as well. "Incoming. Disappear. See if you can keep the media coverage to a minimum."

"Sure, I'll take all of social media offline," drawled Luther.

His grimace expressed how much he missed the old days when a story could be squashed by paying off one nosey reporter. Now everyone with a phone had the ability *and desire* to spread a story to millions.

He gave her a tap on the arm, nodded to Broch, and jogged toward the studio to sniff for whatever substance had driven Timmy to lunacy.

Catriona turned to eyeball the Highlander. He looked as if he'd walked out of a horror movie. In addition to the mess left from wrestling blood-smeared Timmy, a dark scarlet stain spread across the area of his wound.

Broch followed her stare and peered down at his tee. "Ah need tae get a shower."

"We have to talk to the police first."

The officer she'd spotted heading in her direction arrived, having stopped to talk to several other witnesses on his way. He introduced himself and lobbed the usual questions for twenty minutes. It might have gone faster, but he didn't have an ear for Broch's thick Scottish brogue and the Highlander had to repeat every other answer. Exasperated, Catriona began acting as translator. She wasn't sure why, but she'd never had trouble understanding her strapping new intern.

At the end of their interviews, Catriona and Broch headed across the lot to their apartments above the payroll office.

Entering the lower-level, Catriona stopped dead, perplexed by the site of an attractive red-headed woman sitting behind Jeanie's desk.

The woman smiled. "Hello, can I help you?"

"Where's Jeanie?" asked Catriona.

"Oh, I'm sitting in for her for a bit. I'm Anne." The redhead leaned forward with her hand extended and Catriona shook it.

Broch leaned in to shake as well.

"Is she sick?" asked Catriona.

"Nope. Vacation," said Anne. She squinted at them. "Do

you need me to call someone?"

Catriona followed Anne's gaze to Broch's bloody shirt.

"Oh. *No.* We're good. Little dust up on the lot."

Anne nodded. "I heard the sirens. You must be Catriona and Broch?"

"Aye," said Broch, grinning.

Catriona flashed him a sideward glance.

"Yes. We live in the apartments upstairs."

"Apartments?" Anne's head cocked. "Two different apartments or together?"

"Two different," said Catriona, though she didn't appreciate the prying question.

Anne seemed to sense it. She shrugged. "Well, nice to meet you."

"You, too."

Catriona continued to the elevator, grabbing Broch's arm as she moved. He winced as the movement pulled on his wound.

"Sorry," Catriona frowned. "I need to check those stitches."

He grunted. "Ah'm gonna miss Jeanie," he said, glancing at her.

"Me too," she agreed. She wasn't sure how Jeanie had been replaced by a knockout like Anne. She guessed the woman had passed her modeling career days and discovered she couldn't act. A payroll temp job was the next step in her evolution. Though she had to admit, Anne possessed an air of *gravitas* she hadn't noticed in other ex-models she'd met.

Upon reaching their floor, Broch attempted to walk past Catriona's door to his own, but she grabbed his wrist and tugged him back. He yielded to his fate as she unlocked her door and motioned for him to enter.

"After you."

He walked past her into the apartment and turned.

She closed the door.

"Take off your shirt."

Broch did as he was told and pulled his tee over his head, grimacing in pain. As the shirt dropped to the ground, she saw his bandage, tucked beneath his arm beside his massive pectoral muscle, glistening with fresh blood.

"Blech," she said.

"Ah need tae get a shower," he repeated.

"I know, I know. Slow your roll. Let me fix this. You shouldn't even be getting a shower. You shouldn't get the wound wet. You should take a bath."

His eyebrows raised. "We have a bath?"

"No. We don't. Maybe I can tape a plastic bag to this so you can shower. Hold on."

Catriona strode to her en suite bathroom and pulled the plastic blue basket storing her medical supplies from beneath the sink. Returning to the main room, she motioned for Broch to sit on a stool beside her kitchen island.

Gingerly, she peeled back his bandage.

The wound didn't seem as angry as she feared it might be. She wasn't a doctor, but from what she could tell, the stitches had held. All the movement during his struggle with Timmy had encouraged blood to seep through, though, and the area needed a good cleaning. She dabbed the stitched spot with hydrogen peroxide, stroking a cotton ball across his skin to remove the worst of the mess. She ran it across the muscles rippling along his rib cage, feeling like a sculptor as the crusted blood gave way to smooth flesh.

I'm da Vinci and he's my David.

She tittered and his face loomed in her vision, their noses nearly touching as he dipped his neck. "Whit's sae funny?"

She applied more peroxide to the cotton ball, embarrassed he'd caught her daydreaming. "Nothing. Making myself laugh, as usual."

She applied a new bandage, running her hand along his chest to smooth the edges and apply the tape. She probably could have used her fingertips and restrained her strokes to the area immediately surrounding the wound...*but why?*. Better to be thorough, right?

Opening a drawer, she retrieved a gallon freezer bag, snipped away the zip closure, and cut the sides to turn the bag into a piece of plastic sheeting. She scissored it to an acceptable size and then taped it over his bandage.

"This will protect it from the shower. Try not to let the water pound in around the edges."

He nodded and she looked up to find him staring at her.

"What?"

He smiled. "Yer guid at that."

"Bandaging?"

"Aye."

She shrugged. "Thank you. Sean used to get banged up all the time in his younger days. I guess I picked up a few things. I can even do a few stitches if I have to, but I don't think you need any."

Broch reached out with his right hand to stroke her cheek. His feather touch inspired a shiver of pleasure.

Her eyes fluttered shut. When she forced her lids to open, she found the Highlander's gaze on her burned with more than lust—*lust* she might have been able to handle. His desire mingled with a tenderness threatening to unnerve her. She feared if she melted into his arms she'd never solidify again.

She put a palm against his temple and ran her thumb along the scar that crossed his eye. He closed his lids and she leaned in to kiss the one spared by the blow that left the surrounding flesh scarred.

She pulled away, turning to the pile of swabs on the island.

"I made a mess here," she mumbled, tossing tape rolls

into the blue basket.

Broch pulled her hands from her fiddling, the long fingers of his left hand looping around her wrist. He reached around her with his opposite hand to place it on her lower back, sliding it down the curve of her bottom. From his position on the stool, he guided her to stand between his legs.

She didn't resist. He released her wrist and cradled her chin in his palm, his thumb tracing her lips as he leaned in to kiss her.

She returned his kiss, mouth opening as he pressed more deeply. She closed her eyes, her face and arms tingling as her skin flushed, the blood beneath it ignited by his touch.

Catriona tilted back her head to gasp for air and he kissed her neck, cradling her body against the uninjured side of his chest with his massive arm.

"We shuid git merit," he whispered in her ear as his lips brushed there.

Though Catriona had marveled at how well she understood the Highlander's brogue, she missed the whisper. *At first.* Perhaps because she didn't *care* what he'd said, as long as he didn't stop exploring her neck with his mouth.

He pulled her shirt away from her skin to trace her collarbone with kisses. She moaned with pleasure.

Somewhere in the back of her head, a tiny voice sang.

What did he say?

Another section of her brain shouted down that first voice.

Shut up. Just shut up.

She recognized the second speaker. That was her pleasure center. The same voice that talked her into having another glass of wine or accepting dates from hot men she knew would be nothing but trouble.

Usually in that order.

That dumb, fun voice.

Though she fought against it, the more logical side of her mind demanded clarity. It tapped into her sharp memory and looped Broch's mumble over and over until she'd deciphered what he'd said.

No. That couldn't be.

"It sounded like you said we should get *married*," she mumbled, the words mushed as she began to kiss him again.

She dug her nails where his buttocks overlapped the kitchen stool, pulling herself closer to him.

"Ah *did* say that."

She snorted a little laugh—at least *little* enough she wasn't immediately horrified for snorting in the first place. "I'll check my schedule for Tuesday."

His head dipped to kiss a line down her chest toward her breasts. "Na, *noo*. Kin we dae it noo?"

Something about his tone caught Catriona's attention. His question included a whine of what sounded like *deep sincerity*. It wasn't a tone she heard often from herself or her closest friends, but somehow she'd identified the emotion. Perhaps she'd seen it on television.

She stopped and took a moment to clear the lust dust from her brain. *Reluctantly*. She wanted him to *stop talking* and keep using his lips for other things.

He'd been so close...

She pulled back, her hands on either side of his head as if she were dislodging a nursing infant.

Surely, his lips *away* from her skin would help her concentrate.

She slid her hands down his neck to rest on his shoulders.

"Are you asking me to marry you?"

Broch smiled, hazel eyes twinkling like a naughty imp's. He poked her tummy with his index finger. "Of course ah ah'm. Where kin we git merrit? Dae ye'll need a day tae gather yer fowk?" He hooked a finger into the waistband of her jeans and pulled her toward him.

She locked her elbows, bracing herself to keep from being tractor-beamed into his embrace.

She laughed. "Gather my folk? Why? So we can swap chickens?"

Broch's teeth, so white and straight for a man born before modern dentistry, slipped into hiding as his grin disappeared. "Ye hae chickens? Ah'd prefer coos..."

"What are coos? Pigeons?"

"Na, *coos*. Ye *ken*." He slapped a fist on either side of his head and thrust out his index fingers to simulate horns. "*Coos.* Maaae..."

She laughed that his version of *moo* would sound like *may*. She never dreamed a child might *fail* one those pull-toy *The cow goes..?* games as a child.

He'd definitely score in the lowest percentile.

"Ah. *Cows*," she said.

"Aye. Coos. Does Sean have coos?"

Catriona squinted at him.

Wait.

She rubbed her face with her hand. "There are so many problems with what you're saying, I don't even know where to begin."

"Lik?"

"*Lick* the fact I'm not an even trade for a *cow*."

He shook his head. "Oh, na. Yer worth at least *four*."

"Ooh, why didn't you say so earlier? I could have put that on my Tinder bio. *Worth at least four cows.* The boys would have broken their fingers swiping right."

Broch scowled. "Ah dinnae ken—"

She continued. "Second problem—Sean is my only family—except for possibly Fiona and some psycho-dad who's out to kill us both—"

Broch huffed. "Sometimes ye dinnae stop blethering—"

"—and while I'm sure Sean would overlook *your* lack of livestock, what with you being his son and all, that's not the part that's bothering me here."

Broch shook his head. "Ah dinnae give *him* coos, he gives *me* coos."

Catriona gaped. "Wait. You get me *and cows*? He has to *bribe* you to take me?"

Broch shrugged. "Wummin' are expensive."

"Oh. My. *God*."

The past is so messed up.

He stared at her, scratching his head, his right pectoral muscle stretching and bouncing as he moved. She tried not to watch but it was so...

No. Stay focused. The man isn't even interested in you unless you come with livestock.

She snorted to herself again, parking in front of him and putting her hands on her hips to keep from reaching out to *feel* what that muscle felt like when it flexed.

"Okay. Let's call it a draw. You can't help where you're from. I'll drop it if you do."

"Drop whit?"

"The marriage thing. We've known each other less than a month."

"Aye."

"That's too fast."

"Howfur?"

She spaced out the next string of words in a slow staccato beat, using her hand as a puppet to speak them. "I've known you for less than a *month*."

"Sae?"

"So, I'm not going to commit to a lifetime with you without *knowing* you."

"Bit we were aboot tae—" He nodded toward the bedroom.

"Get naked? You want to marry me so we can have sex?"

He scowled. "Aye?"

Catriona took a moment to piece together his logic. "Wait. Are you telling me you *won't* have sex with me unless we're married?"

Broch stared at her, mouth in a grim line, his jawline flexing.

She frowned. "Are *you* a virgin?"

"Nae ah'm nae a *virgin*," he hooted.

She released a long ragged exhale and slapped a hand on his knee. "Whew. I thought maybe that was a thing with you people."

"My people?"

"Time-traveling Highlanders. Nevermind. I get it. You're kidding with me."

One of his eyebrows arched. "Whit?"

"You're kidding that we *have* to be married to..." She hooked a thumb toward the bedroom. "You know."

He rested his open palm on his chest. "Well...*ah* dinnae have tae be merrit. Bit ye—"

Catriona's eyes popped so wide she thought they might drop to the floor.

"But *I do*? Because I'm a girl?"

He shook his head, waving a palm in the air as if he were waxing the side of a car. "Nae, yer takin' this all wrong. Ah'm sayin' ah dinnae think yer a whore."

Catriona gasped, laughing, sending a drop of saliva down the wrong pipe. Placing a hand on an empty barstool, she hung her head, coughing and trying to catch her breath.

"Well, *great*. We agree on that. I don't think I'm a whore either," she croaked.

"Yer nae."

She wrestled the tickle in her throat under control. "No. But for the record, no one uses that term anymore. It's slut-shaming."

"Whit?"

"You shouldn't call girls *whores*."

He gaped. "Ah dinnae!"

"Good."

Broch hooked his mouth to the side. "Are ye sayin' ye *dinnae* wantae tae marry me?"

Catriona titled back her head and rocked it, her mouth hanging open. "I don't *know*. Anything's possible. I barely know you. I need to bring you into the twenty-first century, for one and get to know you better. That process might include *being together*, to know, uh, if we're compatible."

"Howfur cuid we nae be compatible? Is it tae big?" He waved his hand in front of his crotch.

Catriona rolled her eyes. "*No.* Forget what Pete told you." She looked away and mumbled, "Though someday we might have to have a frank conversation about manscaping."

His gaze dropped to her mid-section. "Dae *ye* nae hae the richt bits?"

She scowled. "I have the right *bits*, thank you."

Catriona sighed. Leaning her tush against the back of her sofa, she eyed the bare-torsoed Highlander up and down, wondering how many women would *melt* at a slice of beefcake like him blathering on about *sharing his kip*. She was aching to crawl into his kip, truth be told. She had real feelings for him and he seemed to *return* those feelings. It was nothing short of crazy those feelings were now locked in some strange Highlander chastity zone.

She adored the big lunk, even if he did once eat a tube of toothpaste and nearly tore apart his refrigerator trying to figure out how the "great silver kist" kept things *sae cauld.* If she could build the perfect man from scratch and magically make him come to life, she *still* wouldn't marry her sexy new Frankenstein monster after a *month*. In her experience, it took a good two years to know you were seeing the real person and not the idealized version created in your head.

She once had a friend who'd married a man after a year and nine months of dating. They'd divorced in less than a year. Turned out he had some pretty weird fetishes he could only keep under wraps for two years. Two months after the wedding he'd rolled a fog machine into the bedroom and—

"Cat?"

Catriona snapped from her thoughts. There was Broch, staring at her, waiting for an answer.

Sexy beast.

But hold on...

"There's a lot of fog in Scotland, isn't there?"

His lips parted. "Uh...aye?"

See, there you go.

They hadn't even officially started dating yet. She still had the full two years to get through.

She realized she'd lost the thread of their discussion and hung her head. "Look, I'm sorry. We need to get to know each other better before we even talk about marriage. Honestly Broch, at this point the jury is still out on whether or not you're a full-blown weirdo who can't get over the last Renaissance festival. You've got Sean backing up your story, which goes a long way, but seriously, I can't just marry a time-traveling Highlander or any other man a month after meeting him."

His expression tightened into a ball. "Whit's a Renaissance festival?"

"That's what you took from that?"

He stared at her, waiting for an answer.

She sighed. "It's like a big party where everyone dresses up like they're from the past. Like jugglers and kings and queens and...*you*. They ride horses and joust and eat giant turkey legs."

Broch's expression, which had been blossoming with every new Renaissance character she shared, suddenly collapsed again.

"Ye said all the horses were eaten by the dragons."

Catriona winced. She'd forgotten she'd told him the dragon movie poster downstairs was *real,* and that dragons had eaten all the horses in the world.

Sometimes it was a little too easy to mess with him.

A passing thought, that Broch might not be so fond of *her* in two years, crossed her mind.

I am a terrible person.

She bit her lip. "Um, I might have exaggerated the lack of horses and number of living dragons."

Broch brushed away her confession. "Kin we gae?"

"Where?"

"To a Renaissance festival."

She shrugged. "Oh. Sure. You won't even need a costume."

Broch nodded, pleased with this new development. He slipped from the stool and she found herself in her usual position, staring at the sinews in his neck and the sexy wisps of dark hair curling from his chest to tickle the edges of his throat's v-notch.

"Weel. Ah'm aff tae git mah shower noo."

The mood had been shattered.

As he turned, Catriona reached out to touch his arm.

"About the, uh, kip thing. It doesn't mean I'm not..." She found it hard to say the words. She'd never told anyone she was in love with them before. She wasn't even sure she *was* in love with him, but her feelings were...something like love, weren't they?

Maybe let him go for now. He couldn't get far. He didn't know how to drive, and dragons ate all the horses...

She laughed.

"Whit's sae funny?" he asked, seeming to grow cross.

Her discomfort had made her loopy. "I'm sorry, I—"

Broch gently grasped her arms and stared into her eyes.

"Ah love ye," he said.

She stared back at him. Speechless.

Damn.

He made that look easy.

When she didn't respond, he continued. "Ah want to marry ye. When ye feel the identical way, ye let me ken. Until then—" He motioned to his body. "Ye keep yer hands off this."

She gasped. "Are you *serious*?"

Broch released her and walked to the door.

Catriona watched him go, the urge to chase after him building until her feet moved forward as if they had minds of their own.

"Broch. Wait. Stop. This is some crazy confusion between our—" She couldn't find the words. "—our *worlds*."

Broch paused at the door and glanced back at her, appearing disappointed, wounded and strangely confident, all at the same time. It reminded her of the look movie heroes flashed their heroines before running into the storm to almost certain death.

He's only going to get a shower...

Broch left and closed the door behind him.

Catriona   sighed.

CHAPTER ELEVEN

The phone rang as Sean stepped from his shower. Cursing, he strode to his kitchen, dripping and damning the phone for its control over him.

The caller I.D. told him it was Luther. That didn't bode well. Luther hated cell phones almost as much as he did, and wouldn't call unless there was an emergency.

Bracing himself, Sean answered and listened as his partner shared the horrifying details of Timmy Grey's frenzied attack. The big man assured him Catriona and Broch had handled things as best as could be hoped, and that he was doing what he could to keep the details from the media.

"Drugs?"

Luther grunted. "Don't see how not, but I didn't find any."

"Had the police already searched?"

"No."

Sean sighed. "I'll be there as soon as I can."

He hung up the phone and finished toweling himself dry. He'd hoped to take the day off, maybe putter around the house, but it appeared lazing by the pool wasn't in his stars.

Sean hadn't been in the car five minutes before Parasol

President Aaron Rothstein's assistant Kiki called to tell him action-star Colin Layne had been arrested.

"How? Where?" he asked.

"In public, right after hitting a home run at a charity baseball game for kids. Police swarmed the field."

Sean groaned. He could picture how the rest went. The children's parents' phones popped from their purses and pockets. Movies of the arrest were filmed and would already be posted online.

Sean hadn't seen that one coming. No one in the police department had given him a heads up or requested a pocket change for the information.

"Please tell me he wasn't hurting children."

"No. They found a dead woman under his house."

"What?"

Sean released the air from his lungs as if he'd been punched in the solar plexus. His mind flipped through every detail he'd ever cataloged about Colin Layne, but nothing added up to literal *lady-killer.* Certainly nothing as evil and careless as hiding a body beneath his own house.

He knew Colin fairly well. He'd looked into him when he thought Catriona had caught the actor's eye.

Nothing felt right about this accusation.

Sean realized his mind had been drifting and apologized.

"Where do we stand now?"

Kiki sighed as if she were tired of keeping actors from going to jail, which, no doubt, she was.

"He's arrested. Investigators are on the scene. The studio's lawyers have been dispatched. Aaron wants you to head to Colin's house and see what you can find out there. You *need to get ahead of this thing,*" she said, aping her boss.

"I'm on it."

"Sorry to be the bearer of bad news."

He smiled. "Not your fault, Kiki."

Sean hated breaking his promise to Luther, but Timmy Grey's drama had ended. There was little left for him to do that Luther and Catriona didn't have covered, and he needed to hear the results of Timmy's tox-screen before they planned their next steps.

Sean changed direction and drove to Colin's house in Calabasas. The police had the high-end neighborhood buttoned-down like a sail canvas during a storm, but Sean knew enough of the officers to gain access.

Twenty years on the job had its advantages.

Rolling to a stop a block and a half from Colin's house, Sean couldn't recall the last time he'd seen so many cops in one place. He suspected more than a few officers had responded after hearing who lived there, just for the chance to gawk.

Sean pulled his wallet from his back pocket to retrieve a wad of hundred-dollar bills from the billfold. He slipped the cash into his front pocket and tossed his wallet back into the Jaguar.

Scanning the scene, he recognized a young uniformed officer standing at the perimeter of Colin's home. The kid was a recent transfer from a less glamorous precinct, and Sean remembered him being eager to please. The patches of red dirt on his uniform implied he'd been under the house.

A good place to start.

"Hey Dennis," Sean said, raising a hand to wave.

Dennis's gaze swiveled in his direction. The young man grinned and wiped his palm on his pants to greet Sean with a firm handshake. "Hey, Sean. Crazy stuff going on here. You've got your work cut out with this one."

"What happened?"

Dennis rested his hands on his hips. "Neighbor reported a smell coming from the house. My partner and I got the call—the stench just about knocked us out. I tracked it to the crawlspace and shone a light under there, but couldn't see much. Figured it was a dead animal, but something about it..." He shook his head as if trying to cast away the memory before continuing. "It didn't feel right not to check it out."

"Dead bodies have a smell you don't forget," muttered Sean.

Dennis nodded. "I know that now." He motioned to his filthy uniform. "We rock-paper-scissored it and you can see who lost. I crawled under and found the girl."

"Cause of death?"

"I didn't spend much time playing detective. It was clear she was beyond saving though, I can tell you that."

"How long has she—?" He motioned to the house.

"I heard them say maybe a week."

"Could she have crawled under there herself?"

He shrugged. "She wasn't tied up if that's what you mean."

"Any idea who she is?"

"Name was Cari Clark."

Sean winced, recognizing the name of the missing actress Luther had told him about. The one dating Colin Layne.

That doesn't bode well.

"How'd you identify her so fast?" he asked.

"Techs found her purse."

"Techs under there now?"

"Yeah, they should be wrapping up." He glanced behind him and Sean followed his gaze to see two men in baggy technician coveralls pushing a body-bag-laden gurney toward an ambulance. The ambulance sat in dim solemnity. No flashing lights or speedy driving would save this girl.

Sean patted Dennis on the arm by way of thanks and handed him a business card and a hundred dollar bill with the other hand.

Dennis glanced at the bill. "Aw, man, you don't have to do that. To be honest, I'm a fan of Colin's. I'm hoping he didn't do it."

"It's my pleasure. I appreciate your help."

Dennis looked around and then took the bill with a nod. "You want to hear something creepy?"

Sean leaned in.

"There was a doll next to her purse. A little cowgirl doll. Scared the crap out of me. Something about its face was off."

"What?"

Dennis shrugged. "I'll be honest, I didn't want to look at it too close. You know how dolls are, always lookin' right back at you?"

"Huh. Thanks. If you hear anything else let me know. Number's on the card."

"You got it. Take care, man."

"Will do. Get yourself a shower."

Dennis chuckled and headed for his patrol car.

Sean strolled toward the ambulance. Work done, one of the techs stood balancing himself against the back of the vehicle, grunting as he struggled to rid himself of his dirty coveralls.

Sean caught his eye. "Hey, how you doing?"

"Better than her," he grumbled as the coveralls finally released their grip on his ankle. He sat on the bumper of the ambulance and ran a hand through his sweaty hair.

"I don't know that we've met before. I'm Sean Shaft from Parasol Pictures?" Sean felt himself cringe. He hated saying his full name aloud. When Luther found him on the Parasol Picture lot so many years ago, he'd been groggy and dazed from his time travel. Thanks to his brogue, Luther called him *Sean,* the most Irish name he knew. Unsure of his own name at the time, Sean claimed it. Pressed for a last name, he glanced up and noticed the movie poster for *Shaft* on Luther's office wall.

Sean Shaft was born.

The crime technician shook his hand, seemingly unfazed by Sean's alliterative moniker.

"Vin. I think I've heard of you."

Sean smiled. "Is that a good thing?"

"Depends. You're a fixer, right?"

"Supposed to be. Looks like I'm a little late on this one."

"To cover it up?"

Sean frowned. "No. To stop it before it happened."

Vin balled his coveralls and stuffed them in a bag. "Your boy have a temper?"

"Colin?" Sean thrust his hands into his pockets and thought about the question. Colin was a man's man, not one to take guff, but not an unreasonable hot-head either. He wasn't creepy or evil—not that Sean had seen.

"No. Are you saying she was beaten?"

"Hard to tell. She was pretty discolored at this point."

"You saw something that implied violence, though?"

Vin took a deep breath and exhaled through his nose. Sean recognized the action. It symbolized the moment when people didn't know if they *should* share information, but they were so eager to talk, that they knew they'd be unable to stop themselves.

Sean loved hearing that sigh. He remained quiet so Vin would feel the need to fill the silence.

"I'm not sure if *violence* is the word. I mean, it *is*, but...it's pretty weird."

"How so?"

"She had two cuts, here and here." He put the first two fingers on his right hand on either side of his mouth and dragged them to his chin. "Thin, postmortem."

"Any thoughts on the significance?"

"No, but *intentional*. It didn't happen while dragging her under the house."

"But that's not what killed her?"

"No. Someone hit her in the head with something sharp and strong, like a spike or a pickaxe. Poked a hole in her skull."

Sean grimaced. "Not your everyday weapon, a pickaxe."

"No, but that wasn't even the weirdest part. Someone filled the hole in her head with some kind of foam filler."

Sean opened his mouth to speak and then shut it. Vin continued. "That look on your face. That was me when I saw it. *Why*, right?"

Sean chewed on his lip, pondering the possibilities. "If the killer was trying to save her, he had to know pouring expanding filler into her cranial cavity wouldn't be the way to do it."

"You'd think. It's like something a kid would do to cover up a mistake."

"Desperation maybe?"

Vin shrugged. "Near as I can figure. Doesn't make a whole lot of sense. They'll find out more at the autopsy."

"Sure. Did you see a doll under there?"

Vin's wandering attention snapped back to Sean. "How'd you know about the doll? Is it a thing? Do we have a serial killer on our hands?"

Sean shook his head. "No. Someone told me."

Vin sighed and again dragged his split fingers from his mouth to his chin. "Those lines—same thing on the doll."

"Cuts?"

"Pen or paint or something."

Sean nodded. "Well, thanks, Vin. I won't hold you up." Sean pulled a hundred dollar bill from his pocket and slipped it into Vin's hand as they shook again.

Vin glanced down at the treasure in his palm, smirking. "That's what I heard about you. That you're like Santa Claus around good information." He pushed the money into his pocket. "Thanks. Kid on the way. I could use it."

Sean nodded and headed across the yard.

He wandered around the house grounds as best he could without drawing attention. Although many officers were happy to share information, he didn't want to push his luck and bump into a hardnose.

He walked the perimeter of the neighborhood and stopped at the community's security booth, knocking to catch the guard's attention. A paunchy, middle-aged man straightened from a crouching position inside, appearing sweaty and hassled.

Sean smiled. "Hi. I was wondering if you had video surveillance for the last week?"

The man wiped his brow with the back of his sleeve. "I just finished copying it all to a thumb drive." He thrust the drive through the window at Sean and then retracted the offer. "Wait. You're not the police."

"No. My name's Sean. I work for Parasol Pictures. You are?"

"Jim. That's the studio Colin works for? Parasol?"

Sean nodded and the man pressed the thumb drive against his chest. "This is for the police. They asked me for it."

"Can you make another copy?"

Jim rolled his eyes. "I can. But it's a pain. It takes forever."

Sean reached into his pocket to retrieve another hundred. He held it where the man could see it. "But you *could* do it?"

Jim stared at the money, scratching at his jaw. "It's awfully hot in here. Maybe if it had a friend or two..."

Hand in his pocket, Sean counted off two more bills and produced them.

Jim considered the new offer. "Maybe if *they* had two more friends."

Sean frowned. "Come on, Jim. This is what I have."

The guard sighed. "Fine." He handed Sean the thumb drive and took the money. "I'll make another for the police."

"Thank you."

Sean walked back to his car and replaced the few remaining bills in his wallet.

He stared at the thumb drive and then set it on the seat beside him. A lot of footage to roll through. It was going to be a long day.

For someone. Not me.

Might be time to introduce Broch to videotaped surveillance.

He grabbed his cell phone to call Catriona and share his news.

Chapter Twelve

Catriona stared at the door Broch had shut behind him, her hand still resting on a bloodied clump of cotton balls.

Marry me.

Ha.

That Highlander is crazy...

Her phone rang from its spot on the kitchen counter and she answered to hear Sean's voice, happy for the distraction.

"You have a meeting with Colin Layne this morning?" he asked.

She gasped and looked at her watch, noting for the first time a smear of Broch's blood on her arm. It was nine-fifty. No time for a shower. She licked her thumb and attempted to rub away the mess.

"In ten minutes. I almost forgot—"

"Don't bother."

"No, I can do it. I just have to get changed. There's blood—"

"Cat, he's been arrested."

"Who? Colin? Arrested for what?"

"The murder of Cari Clark."

Catriona gasped and pictured Cari's sister, Dr. Violet. The

air escaped from her lungs in a slow steady stream as she lowered herself to sit cross-legged on the floor.

Damn.

She'd *promised* Dr. Violet she'd find Cari.

Now she felt like an ass twice over. Once for disappointing Broch and once for Violet, and it wasn't even ten o'clock yet.

"I promised Cari's sister I'd find her."

She could hear Sean's disapproval radiating through the phone line. "You shouldn't promise things like that."

"I know. I know. How did Colin supposedly kill her?"

"Looks like a blow to the head. Something sharp and heavy, like a pickaxe."

"A *pickaxe*? She was killed by an old-timey prospector?"

"The tech guessed *pickaxe* from the shape of the wound. I don't know that he meant a pickaxe, *literally*. We'll know more after the autopsy."

Catriona puffed out her cheeks and let the air release with a pop.

They still make pickaxes?

Her mind couldn't wrap around the idea. At least, she guessed, it had been a quick death.

"Why do they think Colin did it?"

"They found her under his house."

"*What?*" Catriona threw her back against the wall with a loud thump. "I guess I can see why they think he's responsible."

"Yes. That's a hard one to explain."

"Do *you* think he did it?"

"I don't know. It's not looking good."

"Was he at the house when they grabbed him?"

"They picked him up at a charity baseball game across town."

"Ouch. Plenty of spectators. That explains the dings on

my phone I haven't had a chance to check. I'd assumed it was about Timmy. The word must be all over town by now."

Catriona had an alert system that warned her when any of their assets appeared in the news or on social media. She'd tried to set the same system up for Sean, but the constant dinging had him ready to throw his phone in the pool within twenty-four hours. He'd disabled it.

"Are they *sure* it's Cari Clark?" she asked.

"They found a purse with the body."

Catriona rested her elbow on her knee and plopped her face into her palm. "This doesn't make sense. Colin *can't* have killed a girl and stuffed her under his house. He's not a killer and he's not stupid."

"Did you two date? Am I remembering that right?"

Arg. She'd been hoping Sean didn't remember that. Catriona felt her face flush with embarrassment and made a series of warbling noises trying to find the right words to explain away her past star-struck stupidity.

"I wouldn't call it *dating*. We had a *flirtation*. Way back when I was an impressionable youth."

"Right. *Way* back then."

"Shush. I can tell you he didn't try to kill me, if that's what you're wondering."

"Did you notice if he owned a pickaxe?"

"*No.* He didn't have an antique weapon collection."

She heard Sean scratching at his scruffy beard.

"Any more news on Timmy?" he asked.

"No, but I haven't had a second to check. I had to patch up Broch. He grabbed Timmy, but the little guy fought like a tiger to get away."

"How's Broch?"

"He's fine. All the struggling started his wound bleeding but the stitches look like they held."

"What's wrong?"

"I just said—"

"No, I can hear it in your voice. Something else."

Catriona groaned. At the mention of Broch, she'd heard the energy leave her voice. Sean must have detected it as well. The last thing she wanted to do was moan about her love life or lack thereof. Especially when they had a murder and a dance judge blitzkrieg to fix.

"Nothing's wrong. Broch and I had a misunderstanding. You don't want to know anymore, believe me."

Catriona knew Sean would offer fatherly advice, but he was still adjusting to the idea of his *real* son traveling through time to potentially date his *adopted* daughter. She hoped her warning would scare him away from the topic.

"Okay. Well, I'll talk to you."

Mission accomplished. Sean suddenly sounded very uncomfortable.

Catriona had a last thought and interrupted his attempt to end the conversation. "Hey, let me ask you. You came from another time. How did you *grow up* here?"

"I was an adult when I arrived."

"No, I mean, how did you adjust to the modern world? Lose your archaic thoughts and habits?"

"Could you be a little more specific?"

"You know, like old-fashioned values. Like thinking women can be swapped for cows."

Sean laughed. "Cows?"

"Okay, forget the cows. Just regular old women's lib. How did you warm up to it?"

There was a pause and then Sean answered. "You."

"Me?"

"Yep. How could I not think of women as equals with someone as strong, independent, and beautiful as you for a daughter?"

Catriona's face grew warm. She couldn't stop smiling.

"Awww... Okay. Now you're embarrassing me."

He chuckled. "Good. Distract yourself with work. Find out about Timmy and I'll keep on Colin for now."

"Will do."

Catriona dropped the phone to her lap and closed her eyes, head pressed against the wall. She had a terrible sense of dread, and it took her a moment to place it.

Dr. Violet. She owed the woman...*something.*

She remained cross-legged on the floor for a few more minutes while Sean's bad news percolated in her mind. She knew there was nothing she could have done to save Cari. From Sean's report, it had sounded as if the girl had been dead before she'd even met Dr. Violet.

If only I hadn't promised to help.

I should know better.

It was a rookie mistake. Sean never would have found himself in this position. She hated that five years into the job, she still had so much to learn.

Catriona stood and stared at the mess of bloody swabs on her counter.

Nope. I cannot deal with that right now.

She had no time to clean and no time to think about her conversation with Broch. It was all too ridiculous to worry about. The practice of throwing in livestock with a woman's hand in marriage was barbaric, but it was the time he grew up in. He didn't know any better.

She chuckled to herself, musing on the livestock dowry. It was a bit like being famous—a woman would never know if her suitor *really* loved her or was just after her father's cows.

She sniffed.

I am losing it.

She knew she'd rather think about cows than face poor, shattered Dr. Violet.

Catriona took a quick shower, pleased to find Broch had

left a drop of hot water in the building. The apartments didn't hold enough hot water for a man making up for a lifetime of icy Scottish river baths.

Catriona threw on some jeans and chose a pair of sneakers over less comfortable footwear. The way her day was going, she felt she needed *comfort over fashion* to survive.

Once dressed, she left the apartment and stood in the hall, staring at Broch's door.

No. He didn't need to come to Violet's. Though she suspected she might miss the shoulder to cry on for the ride back. She needed to do this on her own.

Outside, she slipped behind the wheel of her Jeep and headed for Dr. Violet's. She called Timmy Grey's sister for an update, reckoning his twin would be standing vigil. She'd guessed well. Talia Grey told her the doctors still had her brother sedated while they tested his blood for what might have caused his violent outburst.

So far, his actions hadn't been upgraded to *deadly* outburst. The dancer he'd attacked still breathed. During her vigil, Talia was keeping almost as close a watch on the victim as her brother.

Next, she called Dr. Pete "No-See-Um" Roseum, to lambaste him for teasing Broch about the size of his package.

"Aw, it was just a joke," he said when she reached him, but he couldn't stop laughing.

"Broch's not from...*here*," she said, avoiding sharing all Broch's truths.

Pete scoffed. "He's got a freakin' baby's arm down there. What about *my* feelings? You think seeing that didn't ruin *my* day?"

Catriona began to giggle. "Be *nice,* Pete. He's finding his feet."

"Then they must be smaller than the rest of him because you can't miss his—"

"Goodbye, Pete."

"Good day to you."

Still laughing, Catriona hung up. For a moment she'd almost forgotten the grim task ahead of her. She could always count on Pete to make her laugh.

Catriona reached Violet's house, pulling to the curb just as the doctor closed her front door and began walking to her car.

Violet took a moment to glare at Catriona through the passenger window of the Jeep. Catriona could tell the police had already made contact. Her eyes were puffy from crying.

Catriona caught up to Violet as she opened the door of her car.

"Dr. Clark—"

Violet whirled to point a finger in her face. "You *said* you'd find her for me. You *said* you'd bring her home *safe*."

Catriona's heart broke. She wrung her hands, finding it hard to formulate the words to describe how *terrible* she felt. "I'm so sorry. She—" Catriona cut short and stared at her toes, knowing nothing she said would make Violet feel any better. She wanted to offer her support, but she didn't want to tell the grieving woman where they found the body or how long her little sister had been dead. The more she talked, the more likely the doctor would begin to ask questions. The last thing Catriona wanted to do was mention the pickaxe-shaped wound.

Steeling herself, she looked up to meet the woman's pained gaze. She set her jaw, determined to push through her feeling of discomfort. No amount of embarrassment or shame could come close to equaling the pain Violet had to be feeling.

"I'll find out what happened," she said. The words sounded weak.

Violet huffed and looked away, her hand falling to her side as if the weight of holding her accusatory index finger aloft had been unbearable. Her voice lost its anger and fell to a low murmur. "No, you won't. You'll protect that man. That's your job, isn't it?"

"No—" Again Catriona found herself tongue-tied.

Well, yes. But no—

Violet dropped into her car and slammed the door before Catriona could say another word. The doctor pulled from the driveway, and Catriona watched her go, helpless to do anything else.

Well, that went well.

The horrible truth of Violet's departure occurred to her as the woman drove from view.

She's on her way to identify the body.

She couldn't blame the grieving sister for her anger, though she wished she'd been able to talk to her. Dr. Violet might know more than even *she* was aware—might know of other boyfriends or bad blood between Cari and other people in her life. Maybe when the doctor had time to work through her shock they could talk. Catriona *did* want to make things as right as she could, even if nothing she did could bring back Cari.

Catriona walked toward her vehicle, recalling the few memories she could summon about her short flirtation with Colin Layne.

Could he have killed a girl?

He was a player, of that she was certain. His fondness for the ladies was both what drew him to her and what ultimately kept them from getting very far. Physically, Colin was utterly delicious, with bright blue eyes and a wiry, made-for-movies body that played a lot taller on screen than his actual five-foot-ten. His attentions had been flattering—almost overwhelmingly so for a twenty-three-year-old, new-on-the-job studio fixer. But on her way to meet him where he was shooting on the backlot, she'd stumbled across a beautiful redhead sobbing to her friend about the brisk love affair she'd been unceremoniously ousted from the day before. She'd almost passed the two women when she heard the name of the cad who'd dumped the ginger.

Colin Layne.

The serendipitous eavesdrop had been enough to snap Catriona from her smitten-kitten phase. She'd realized how close she'd come to becoming another footnote in his future autobiography.

She was flattering herself to even imagine she'd get *that* billing.

She'd admonished herself for the mistake that might have been. She and Colin would be working on the same lot for years to come. What had she been thinking? That *she'd* be the woman he spurned all others for, even as they threw themselves at his feet, day after day?

Sean had warned her not to get involved with any of the assets, and she'd come very close to breaking that rule after a mere three weeks on the job. Colin had pounced on her as if she were fresh meat and she'd nearly rolled over and exposed her throat for him.

Still...

Colin might be a dog, but he didn't seem like the type to kill a woman with a pickaxe. He'd also never be so stupid as to stuff the body under his own house. Even if, in the heat of the moment, it had seemed like a good temporary solution, he wouldn't have left it there for a *week* while he played charity softball games. Anyone who'd ever watched a single episode of *CSI* or *Dateline* would know the California heat would soon cause an exposed body to stink. The critters would find the rotting flesh and then there was no telling what might be dragged into the light...

Catriona stopped with her hand poised on the handle of her car door.

Anyone would know that.

Maybe that was the point.

Every murderer in the world tried to hide evidence, one way or another. Put the body in the ground, take it out to the desert, chop it up and throw it in a dumpster somewhere far from their house...

No one would leave it under their house.

Unless they wanted it to be found.

Was someone setting Colin up? She needed to find out who his enemies were.

She called Sean.

"I have an idea—"

"Hey, glad you called. I forgot to mention, I need you and Broch to go through all the camera footage for Colin's community gatehouse. I think someone is setting him up."

Catriona growled. "Well, you just took all the fun out of my big announcement. It hit me that no one would stash a body under their house unless they *wanted* to be caught."

"I beat you to that one."

"Well, we don't know if you beat me *officially*... how long ago did you come up with that theory?"

"Before I called to tell you about the body."

Catriona sniffed. "Oh. Okay, fine. You win." She turned her head. "Barely."

"I know. But I do think we *all* need to get our heads around this."

"Which *this*? You have to be more specific today."

"No, I don't. That's my point. I just got a call from Teena Milagros. She's received a death threat."

Catriona recognized the name of the studio's triple threat. Teena was a singer, dancer, and actress... a bit of a looney tune as well. "You think Colin, Timmy, and Teena are all connected somehow?"

"I don't know, but things are starting to feel a little forced at this point."

"You think someone's out for Parasol?"

"It's a possibility we can't ignore. Is Broch with you?"

"No. He had to get a shower after his ordeal with Timmy and showers are like a religious experience for him. I left him to it while I went to talk to Violet."

Sean uttered a low grunt that expressed his appreciation for how difficult talking to Violet must have been. "How'd that go?"

"Not well. The police had already gotten to her though, so at least I didn't have to be the maker of false promises *and* the bearer of bad news."

"Don't beat yourself up. You didn't kill her sister."

"I know. It still sucks."

"What about Timmy? Have you talked to him yet?"

"I called his sister. He's still sedated, should come out of it soon."

"Okay. Gather Brochan. My office in half an hour."

"Will do."

"I think I have a theory on why the hole in her head was full of expanding foam."

"Great...wait, *what*?"

Sean hung up and Catriona stared at her phone.

What did he say?

She looked at her watch to find it was only eleven o'clock.

It felt as though she'd already lived a lifetime.

CHAPTER THIRTEEN

Edinburgh, Scotland 1833

"Fiona?"

Brochan stood at the edge of the forest, scanning for signs of life. Fiona had finished her meal at the tavern and asked him to rendezvous in four days to meet her friends.

He hadn't committed to the meeting then, but he'd been unable to stop thinking about the larcenous vixen. He knew from the moment he awoke that morning he'd be unable to ignore her invitation. It had something to do with her name, certainly—that she should carry the label forced upon his love by her murderous father. Fiona wasn't an uncommon name in Scotland, but was it so common amongst American girls?

He needed to find out more.

"Fiona?" he called again, the dense forest seeming to swallow the sound.

Something moved in the shadow of the trees. A head poked from behind a great pine. Broch trained his gaze on it, and a moment later more shadows stirred until four people manifested from the gloom. They drew together as they walked toward him from their hiding places, with Fiona leading the pack. Behind her walked two men, one of average size and one stouter fellow, both trailed by a smaller figure he suspected to be another girl dressed in men's leggings, much like Fiona had worn during their midnight introduction.

Today, Fiona modeled a dark blue and red striped earasaid fashioned as a skirt below and tied beneath her breasts with a brass buckle. The top half of the cloth draped behind her back, wrapping over her shoulders and pinned beneath her throat. Broch recognized the carved images of stags in the brass buckle around her middle as his neighbor's wife's favorite adornment. She'd worn the item many times. She was a plain woman and his father had joked the buckle seemed overwhelmed by the job of improving her appearance.

The earasaid itself appeared familiar as well, though he couldn't recall which neighbor might have *donated* the item to his light-fingered dinner guest.

Fiona strode forward to meet him as the others slowed to remain in the trees' shadows. The average-sized man spat, and even in the dim light, Broch could tell none of them seemed eager to receive him as their guest.

"Brochan," said Fiona, her arms outstretched. She seemed very different than the hungry creature he'd watch gobble meat scraps at the tavern. Her cheeks appeared fuller, her color better.

"Ye look well," he said.

She smiled, dazzling white teeth flanked by dimply-laugh lines on either side. "We've had time to learn the area. I feel more at home now thanks to the kindness of strangers like you."

He eyed her dress. "Ah think that belt wid feel mair at hame in mah neighbor's hoose."

She glanced down at the stags and giggled as if his accusation of thievery had been the funniest joke she'd heard in some time. She reached for his hand and pulled him forward.

"Come meet my friends."

He allowed himself to be led.

"This is Harry," Fiona motioned to the stout man. His head, nestled in the fat of his neck, wobbled in a subtle sign of greeting. Broch guessed him older than himself, perhaps in his mid-thirties. He seemed too old to be running with a pack of young thieves, but nothing about his disheveled clothing implied his life had gone as planned.

Fiona gestured toward the person Broch suspected to be female, though standing closer to the creature hadn't made him more confident in his guess.

"This is Greer. She does most of our cooking and camp chores." Greer raised her gaze to steal a glimpse of him before looking away. Her teeth hung from her mouth in such a fashion it would be impossible to tuck them away without considerable effort.

Fiona leaned close to him and whispered. "She doesn't speak much."

He nodded as she turned her attention to the last man. "This is Mathe. He took me into the group when I found myself alone here in Scotland."

Mathe stared at Broch with hard eyes and spat again. Broch watched the foamy gob land a foot from his boot. Mathe continued to stare into his eyes as if silently daring him to complain.

Brochan took a deep breath to keep his anger at bay. "Hullo."

Without another word, the three bandits turned and faded into the forest. Fiona remained at Brochan's side.

She offered him a sheepish smile.

"None of them are very talkative."

"How come did ye ask me tae come 'ere?"

She laughed and put her fingers on his elbow, stroking

down his forearm until she took his hand in hers. "Maybe I needed someone to talk to."

He cocked an eyebrow. "Aye. Ah've met yer friends. Ah could see that."

She locked her arm in his. "You seem like you need a break from your toils as well."

Broch frowned, ashamed that his dissatisfaction with his life might appear so obvious to a stranger. When Fiona asked him to meet her at this place, far on the edge of town, her mysterious plan had excited his blood. Foolish, he knew, that a clandestine meeting could raise in him such a thrill, but true, nonetheless.

Fiona guided him behind the path of the others and Brochan fell into step beside her.

"Ah dinnae hae any plan tae become a thief," he warned.

She shrugged. "We only take what we need to survive."

His gaze fell to her midsection. "Ye wid die withoot that buckle?

She tittered. "You'd rather I walk around naked?"

He looked away and let her comment die on the vine. He knew poisonous fruit when he saw it.

"Why dinnae ye find work?" he asked. He hoped changing the subject would erase the picture conjured in his mind by her naughty comment.

"*You* work. Are you happy?" she asked.

Broch took a deep breath. "Ah wis."

"What changed?"

He shrugged. Catriona had changed everything in his world, but he wasn't ready to share his precious memories of her.

Fiona released his arm, spinning away to jump in front of him, blocking his path. "Stay here with us."

He shook his head. "Ah tellt ye, ah'm nae a thief."

"So don't *thieve*. You can be our muscle. Or a watcher."

He didn't answer.

With a flourish she took his arm once more, leading on until they reached the group's camp. The others had found places around a large fire pit. Above it, a small deer roasted on a spit. Greer fussed with it, turning it to keep the cook even.

Two horses stood tied to a tree and Fiona stopped to stroke the neck of one.

"At least spend the night. We have a barrel of ale and Mathe shot a stag this morning. We're going to have a feast."

Broch considered the offer. It wouldn't hurt to stay. The meat did smell good and he had nothing awaiting him at home except the same routine he walked through every night.

"Mebbe a while—"

The gelding Fiona stroked flattened his ears and kicked out with its hind leg, striking the other horse. The mare squealed and circled the tree to escape her attacker.

Fiona jumped away, falling into Broch's arms. He swept her away from the animal.

"Dammit Fiona, ah tellt ye tae stay away fae the horses." Mathe sprang from his seat and moved to calm the beasts.

Fiona looked up from her place in Brochan's arms, grinning. "I guess I don't have a way with *some* beasts."

Staring down into her comely face, Brochan felt a stir in his loins. He released her and took a step back, nodding toward the makeshift spit.

"If ye lik', ah could make ye a proper spit."

Fiona rolled her eyes. "That would be nice. Come sit with me."

He could tell she was flirting with him. It didn't seem a terrible thing except for everything about Fiona felt like trouble.

A passing thought of Catriona bounced through his head and made his chest tighten with guilt and regret.

She isnae coming back.

Why couldn't he accept that?

Brochan found himself a seat by the fire and Fiona scooped him a tin mug of ale from their stolen barrel. Chubby Harry's mood changed with each mug he quaffed. After wobbling to the barrel for his fourth helping, he regaled the Highlander with tales of the group's exploits. He shared the places they'd robbed, what they'd taken, and most excitedly, the ways they'd nearly been caught. He told Brochan how they'd begun to think they were cursed when Fiona crept into his blacksmith shop and he'd given her a meal. That same night, Greer and Mathe had stumbled onto the ale and a cache of vegetables that had kept them fed until Mathe scored the deer.

Harry grinned and took a swig before continuing in his own Sassenach accent. "Fiona says you're our good luck charm."

Broch hooked his mouth to the right. "Ah dinnae ken aboot that."

"Tell me more about blacksmithing."

"Lik' whit?"

"I heard you tell Fiona you could pound us a proper spit. How would you do that?"

Brochan fell into a lengthy discussion about what it would take to fashion a spit and how one builds a sword from scratch. By the time he was finished talking, he found Fiona had left his side and now sat beside Mathe. The two spoke in low tones. Fiona did most of the speaking, smiling and flashing looks at Broch as she did so. Each time her eyes wandered, Mathe grew more agitated.

Broch found it difficult to continue his story with Harry.

Aye. She's trouble.

Fiona cast a final furtive glance in Broch's direction before standing. As she rose, she smoothed her hand along Mathe's arm. The man stiffened. His hand shot up to grasp her wrist, holding her in place beside him.

"Let go," she said.

Mathe sneered his grip tightening, his eyes locked on Brochan's.

Fiona tugged. "Let go. You're hurting me."

Certain Mathe's stare was meant to provoke, Brochan set down his mug.

"Let her gae."

Mathe stood, his hand still clamped around Fiona's wrist. "Or whit?"

Brochan rose from the log on which he'd been perched. "Or ah'll teach ye some manners."

He heard Harry mumble, *Here we go again*, but didn't have time to wonder what the man meant. Mathe jerked Fiona toward him, holding her in front of him like a shield. His filthy fingers kneaded her porcelain throat and her eyes flashed with fear.

Brochan took a step forward.

"Let her gae."

Mathe squeezed harder and Fiona gasped for air.

"Nae one wants ye here. *Ye* gae."

Broch smiled. "Ah ken ye need tae use her as a shield. Ah'm much stronger than ye."

Mathe's nostrils flared. He threw Fiona to the side and she yipped as she struck the ground. Her hand on her throat, she scrambled away from Mathe, staring at Broch with pleading eyes.

Broch widened his stance.

Mathe wasted no time.

Roaring, he launched himself at Brochan.

The Highlander stepped back with his right foot to brace for the attack. Though Mathe was a smaller man, Broch knew his estimation of the thief's strength had fallen shy of the mark the moment they grappled. He could overpower the thief, but Mathe's smaller, wiry frame allowed him to move with the agility of an adder. Each time Broch thought he'd captured him, Mathe appeared in a new place, peppering him with punches.

"C'moan ye great stupid lump," screamed Mathe.

Broch absorbed a smack to the jaw and moved with the punch to lessen the blow he couldn't avoid. As his head turned, he spotted Fiona leaning by a tree, watching the two men fight with great amusement. Her expression could be described as nothing less than *glee*.

Ah've fallen for it.

Fiona had goaded Mathe into the fight. Brochan knew it as sure as he knew his own name, for he'd seen the behavior many times before. His friend Gavin had managed to date every such woman in town until Broch felt his part-time job was ensuring his less athletic friend wasn't pounded to death by jealous husbands and lovers.

Broch remained doubled over, pretending to be shaken by Mathe's blow. When his foe moved forward, he spun to grab him. Caught off guard, Mathe's evasive maneuver proved ill-timed, and Broch wedged the man's head into the crook of his elbow, choking him. He turned Mathe so he was facing Fiona.

"Ye see the lassie?" He whispered in Mathe's ear.

Mathe continued to struggle, so Broch tightened his grip.

"Ah *said*, dae ye see the lassie there?"

Mathe's eyes grew droopy, so Broch eased his chokehold. The man's eyes bulged once more and then darted to his. Broch could feel him attempting to nod in the affirmative.

"Ye see her smilin'?" he asked.

Mathe nodded again.

"She's smiling fur she git us tae battle, isnae she? Did we hae a quarrel?"

Mathe shook his head.

"Sae dae ye'll want tae keep fightin' fur her amusement

lik' dancin' bears, or dae yi'll waant tae halt?"

"Stop," croaked Mathe.

Broch responded with one sharp nod. "Aye. Guid choice. Ah'm goain tae let ye gae."

Mathe nodded and Brochan released his grip on the man. Mathe stumbled away with as much aplomb as he could manage. He glared at Fiona and strode to the far side of the clearing, rubbing at his throat.

Brochan walked to Fiona, massaging his jaw where Mathe had connected with one of his better shots. The amusement had left Fiona's expression. She looked like a little girl who'd had her favorite toy stolen.

"Ah'm goan tae gae," he said.

Her petulant scowl deepened. "Why?"

"Ah shouldnae be 'ere and ah dinnae appreciate bein' used."

"Used? What are you talking about?"

Brochan frowned. "Mathe hud na idea whit he wis mad aboot. The wrestle wis yer idea."

Fiona gaped. "No, it wasn't. He's jealous. He's embarrassed to say—"

Broch turned his back to her and nodded to the others. "Ta, fur yer hospitality. A'm aff tae be headed hame noo."

The three thieves nodded to him from their various perches, including Mathe, who'd flopped to the ground beside the horses. No one seemed shocked or disappointed by his plans to leave.

He glanced back at Fiona. "Cheers. Guid luck with yer endeavors."

Brochan strode into the forest, knowing he'd stayed too long. He'd also failed to pay close attention to the path he'd traveled with Fiona upon arriving. Once he felt he had reached the limit of the camp's view, he paused to find his bearings. Wandering the woods for the rest of the night would be adding insult to injury. He'd already been fooled once.

He'd picked his direction when he heard footsteps behind him. They fell too heavy and regular to be those of a squirrel.

"Show yerself," he said, tensing for what he suspected might be Mathe's revenge. The odds Fiona had goaded the wee man into reclaiming his honor weren't low.

"It's me."

Fiona walked from the shadows into a beam of tree-filtered moonlight, striking in the bluish glow of midnight.

She approached until she stood inches from him.

He couldn't find the will to move.

She placed both her hands on his chest and they stood that way, gazes locked, her palms rising and falling with his breath.

"Don't go," she whispered.

He realized what had so bewitched him about her appearance. Her beauty, certainly, deserved attention. But in the dim light, ghostly porcelain skin aglow, she looked like Catriona's twin.

He put a hand on each of her hips. She took it as an invitation and rose onto her toes to kiss him. The moment before her lips touched his, he pulled back and turned his head.

"Na," he whispered.

She flattened her stance and took a step back. "Are you still mad about the fight? I'm sorry. I swear I didn't encourage him."

Unaware he'd been holding his breath, Brochan found himself in distress and inhaled, feeling light-headed.

"Ah need tae gae."

She grabbed his arm. "Stay with me."

"Ah cannae."

She crumpled his shirt with her right hand, balling it in her fist. "Why? Am I not pretty enough for you?"

He huffed a little laugh. "Na. It isnae that. Yer beautiful. Ye ken that."

"Then what?"

He swallowed and wished for the power to change the woman holding his wrist into the woman he longed to hold. The woman he'd lost.

Part of him wanted to take this woman here and now. She wasn't Catriona, but perhaps she could help him be rid of her specter...

He grabbed Fiona and pulled her toward him, his lips close to hers.

She tilted back her head. "Kiss me."

His breathing came faster.

"Kiss me. *Take me*," she urged.

He released her with a grunt of frustration, spinning away, hands held out to his sides.

"Ah cannae."

There was silence between them as he regained his composure. Running his hand through his hair, he turned back to find her staring at him, her head cocked.

"You have a love?" she asked.

He nodded. "Ah dae."

"And she's better than me? Fairer?"

"She's deid."

"What?"

"My Catriona's deid."

"Catriona..."

Though it seemed impossible, Fiona's skin grew paler.

"Whit's wrong?"

"Tell me about her."

An image of Catriona teasing him outside his blacksmith shop flashed in Brochan's mind and he smiled. He hadn't realized how much he needed to speak of his time with her until that moment.

"She looks a lot lik' ye, with stormy eyes and a mind full of fire and fancy."

"Where did you meet her?"

"In the pub. She wis with her da."

He thought he heard Fiona gasp. "What did he look like? Her father?"

"Thin. Eyes like ice. Bones as sharp as knives and a cruel temper to wield them."

"Why do you say that? That he was cruel?"

"He beat Catriona. Ah saw him do it. And he called her by a name not hers."

"What name?"

"Yours. Fiona."

Fiona raised a hand to cover her mouth. "You said she's dead?"

"Aye."

"How did she die?"

"Her da shot her. Ah think his plan wis to kill me but—" It hurt him to recall the memory. The guilt he felt, that she took the shot meant for him, was a weight he'd borne every day since her death.

Fiona moved forward and grabbed his shirt again, this time in both fists. She pulled at it, her jaw clenched tight as her face drew close to his.

"You saw her die?"

Broch took her wrists in his hands to stop her from tearing the fabric. It felt as if she were trying to climb him, to crawl inside his head and pull the answer from him.

"Whit's wrong with ye?" he asked.

"Did you see her die?"

"Aye, she died in my arms."

The tension on his shirt ceased as Fiona's grip released. He let her wrists slip from his fingers and her arms dropped to her side.

"That's impossible," she whispered.

"Ah wish it wis. Ah buried her myself."

Fiona's head shot up. "You buried her? *Here*?"

"Nearby. My friend offered her a lair."

Fiona took a few steps away from him. He thought he heard her whisper.

"Impossible."

When Fiona finally looked up from her thoughts, her confusion seemed to have passed. A saucy smirk curled the corner of her mouth and she ran her tongue across her upper lip, like a lioness preparing for a meal.

She walked forward to slide her arms on either side of Broch's hips. Placing her hands on his rump, she pulled him toward her with one sharp jerk. He held his hands in the air.

"Let me help you forget her," she murmured. She reached up to grab his arm, pulling it down toward her until she could grasp his wrist. Cupping the back of his hand, she guided it down to place his palm against her bosom.

Broch felt his body reacting to her proximity without his permission. Again his head swam as if her perfume muddled his senses. He pulled his hand from her breast and took a step back.

"Git away fae me, wummin'."

She ignored him and stepped forward again, shifting from seductress to lovesick girl. She clasped her hands together beneath her chin, pleading. "Please. You'll see. You'll love me better—"

He shook his head, as much to deny her as to clear it. "Ah willnae. Yer some kind of a witch." He took another step back and stumbled, catching himself against a tree.

Fiona's mood shifted a third time as Broch watched her fury rise. Again she stepped close to him. Blocked by the tree, he could no longer retreat. She squelched her threatening posture by relaxing her expression, but her fists remained balled at her sides. "Take me. I *command* you."

As if a spell had been broken, Broch laughed, and the sound of his amusement sharpened his senses. A fog lifted from his mind and he saw Fiona for what she was, a spoiled girl, accustomed to having her way with men.

Why had ah been sae frightened of this lassie?

Her eyes flashed with anger. "You can't resist me."

He sniffed. "Och, ah can and ah hae—"

Her hand shot out and slapped him, hard, across the face. Surprised by the blow, he barely snapped from his shock in time to catch her other hand as it arced through the air to strike his opposite cheek.

They remained frozen, he holding her hand inches from his face, glaring at one another.

"I'm here," she said, her voice low. "She's *dead*."

Brochan felt his anger rise and he released her wrist, dashing it downward.

"Aye. Bit she's still a better wummin' than ye."

He turned and strode through the forest toward home.

No   footsteps   followed.

CHAPTER FOURTEEN

Broch sat up with a gasp and looked around his apartment.

Hollywood. Nae Scootlund.

He took a deep breath and imagined he could still smell the lingering scent of Fiona's stolen perfume. He'd dreamt about her again. Ultimately, he'd left her behind in that forest. He hoped that would be the end of his memories of her. Something about the woman inspired a sense of foreboding.

Broch rubbed his eyes and realized he'd been sleeping on his sofa. He'd been getting dressed, trying to decide if today would be a kilt day or a pants day after his shower. He'd only meant to rest for a moment.

Glancing down, he noticed he'd made it as far as donning the comfortable, grippy underwear Catriona had bought for him. He liked the way they kept his nether parts *just sae.*

He pulled at the waistband with a hooked thumb, enjoying the springing feeling of the fabric as he strolled into the kitchen to check the great metal kist for food. After he'd dismantled the refrigerator in search of its secret for keeping food cold, Catriona had called a man to come and put it back together again. When Broch asked the man for the secret, he'd been told the food stayed cold thanks to "Freon." Broch didn't love the explanation but it wasn't worth breaking the kist again to find the real magic yet. He didn't like being without cold food.

He grabbed an apple and bit it in two before turning on the television the way Catriona had shown him. He liked the television. It was a great way to learn about his new world and be entertained as well.

A dancing man appeared on the screen, gyrating his hips for a crowd of screaming women. Slowly, but with great flourish, he began to remove his clothes.

The women went *wild*.

Broch took another bite from his apple.

Ah didnae ken the lassies lik'd that.

Soon, the man had stripped down to his underwear. The man's underclothing looked as though they were made from the same springy material as his own, though the dancer's were much *smaller*. They barely did their job, which seemed impractical.

He searched the remote for the 'Info' button and pressed it to force the title of the program to appear.

Magic Mike.

Hm. Magic. Mibbie his dancin' is casting a sort o' spell o'er the lassies.

He stood and was about to head for the bedroom to finish dressing when he heard a knock on the door. Spinning on his heel, he followed the sound, opening the door to find Catriona standing in the hall. Her gaze dropped to his underwear.

"Broch, you can't answer the door in your skivvies."

He stepped back to allow her entry. "Bit it wis whit ah wis wearing."

"I understand that, but you need to put on *more* clothes before you answer the door. If Jean or the new girl came up here and you answered like that, you'd give the poor women heart attacks."

She tossed her purse on his kitchen counter and stretched her neck from side to side.

"I'm having a terrible day," she mumbled. "Get dressed. We have to go to Sean's office."

He grinned.

"Why are you looking at me like that?"

Broch began to gyrate his hips in slow, tight circles, doing his best to imitate the men he'd seen on the television.

"Ye lik' this?" he asked.

She blinked at him.

"Why do you look like you're working an invisible hula hoop?"

Turning his chest to the wall, he shook his bum, sliding down the paint into a squat and then standing again.

"Aye?" he asked, waggling his eyebrows.

Catriona squinted, her lips pressing tighter until she laughed out loud.

Broch stopped shaking and tried to remember if the women in the movie had *laughed*. They'd been *smiling* but it wasn't *laughter*...

He doubled down and gyrated to the thumping rhythm playing in his head. "Dinnae be embarrassed how it makes ye feel."

He moved toward her and she put out her palms, bracing her elbows to stop his progress. He settled his ribs against them.

"Is it tae much fer ye?"

Catriona's face turned red from giggling. A tear rolled from one eye.

It wasn't the effect he'd been hoping for.

He put his hands behind his head like he'd seen the men on the television do and made his pecs bounce, once after the other.

"Ye want to marry me noo?"

Catriona howled with laughter and, appearing weak in the knees, turned away to support herself on his kitchen island.

"Stop, please. You're killing me..." she said between snorts.

He straightened and put his hands on his hips, scowling. "It's nae workin'?"

Catriona sniffed, wiping tears from her eyes. "*No,* you big doofus. You're not going to *dirty dance* me into marrying you. Go get dressed. We have to be at Sean's office in fifteen minutes."

Broch scowled. "Ye *will* give in."

She rolled her eyes, still seemingly unable to keep from tittering. "Whatever."

Broch stormed toward his bedroom. Inside, he stared at his bed until he had an epiphany.

The man on the television had a move he hadn't tried. It made the girls *scream* with desire.

Broch turned to face his door and backed until his heels clipped his bedside table.

"Catriona."

"What?"

"Come staun here next tae the windaes."

Catriona poked her head into the bedroom. "What? Why?"

He waggled a finger toward the windows. "Over there. Staun over there in front of me. In the far neuk."

Catriona arched an eyebrow. "I'm starting to think that trip through time injured your brain."

"Just dae it."

Catriona walked to the far corner of the room. She turned to face Broch through the open door of his bedroom. "Here?"

"Aye."

Broch took a deep breath.

Springing off his heels, he bolted toward her.

If he judged his speed and timing correctly, he'd slide right to her feet, where he'd ask her to marry him again...

She willnae be able tae resist.

As he crossed the threshold from the bedroom into the main living area, he dropped to his knees to slide across the floor like the magic men had done. He opened his arms, preparing to glide to Catriona's feet.

His knees jammed on the wooden floor.

They did not slide.

He saw a flash of Catriona gasping in horror, her hand rising to her mouth before his forward momentum abruptly stopped and he fell face forward, the ground rising to meet his face at an alarming speed. He caught himself with the side of one hand a second before his face hit the ground full force, but with his awkward position, he couldn't cease *all* his momentum. Smacking his forehead against the floorboards, he ended on his knees with his cheek and nose pressed against the wood, his ass hiked high in the air.

Catriona spoke from behind her hand.

"You did *not* just do that."

Broch groaned and slid his legs out straight behind him until he lay with his belly on the ground.

"Ow."

She snorted her signature laugh. "Are you okay?"

"Aye."

Catriona reached down as he pushed himself up, allowing her to help him to his feet.

She glanced at the television where a man and a woman stood talking. "Is that *Magic Mike*?"

He wiggled his nose left to right to check it for breaks. "Aye."

Catriona slipped her hands around his middle to hug his good side. He wrapped his arm around her.

"You're adorable. An *idiot*, but adorable," she said, stretching up to kiss his cheek.

He grunted and pecked the top of her head.

Patting him on the chest, she headed for the door. "Go get dressed before you rip out your stitches. We have to go."

He took a step toward the bedroom and stopped. "Och, ah with all mah dancin', ah almost forgot—"

"What?"

"Ah dreamt of Fiona again."

Catriona hooked her mouth to the side. "Are you trying to make me jealous now?"

"Na. But ah thought you'd lik' tae ken she tried tae seduce me."

"Seems that's a habit with her."

"Aye. Bit ah didnae touch her."

"No?"

"Na. Tellt her tae leave."

"Yeah?"

"Aye."

He could see Catriona struggling to hide her emotions, but she seemed pleased.

"Huh," was all she said before leaving and closing the door behind her.

From the hall, he heard a joyous whoop and grinned.

He'd have to work on the dancing.

CHAPTER FIFTEEN

Broch and Catriona entered Sean's office to find Luther sitting in his usual spot in the corner of the sofa. That side of the ancient leather furniture sat lower than the opposite side, thanks to the big man's preference.

Catriona pulled the chair away from Sean's desk so she wouldn't feel as if she'd been called to the principal's office. Broch followed suit and slid a chair beside hers.

Sean straightened behind his desk.

"Okay, we need to get a handle on this."

"What do we know so far?" asked Catriona.

Sean looked at Luther. "Anything new on Colin?"

The big man rubbed his bald head. "Nothin' yet. Still working on going through the surveillance footage. You two can help me with that after this." He nodded to Catriona and Broch.

"Whoopie," mumbled Catriona.

Sean tapped a pen against his desk. "The time of death hasn't been narrowed down, and I don't know if Colin is going to have an alibi for all of it. He says he hasn't been home in a couple of days. He's been sleeping at the home of a..." Sean paused and glanced at Catriona.

Catriona felt her lip curl as if the smell of dead fish had suddenly filled the room. "Oh *please* don't think Colin's romantic life has any effect on *me*. That is ancient non-history."

Sean flicked his wrist as if shooing away a fly. "No, I know. Anyway. Hopefully, the girl can provide him with a solid alibi."

"Did he ken the deid lassie?" asked Broch.

Sean nodded. "They'd been dating, but not so seriously that he found it odd when he didn't hear from her for a few days."

"Or so seriously he wasn't staying at some other girl's house when she was killed," mumbled Catriona.

She looked up to find Sean staring at her. "Not that I *care*."

Catriona glanced at Broch and then leaned her elbows on her knees to address Sean. "So, to be clear—you're saying a man and woman can sleep together, without being married?"

Sean scowled. "Uh, why does your question fill me with fear?"

"No? So he was paying her for sex?"

"What? *No*. I said they were dating."

"But she was the sort of girl he could never marry, of course."

Sean glanced at Luther. The big man shrugged.

He returned his attention to Catriona.

"What the hell are you going on about?"

She turned her palms skyward. "Oh, you *know*. If she was sleeping with him and they weren't married, she must not be the sort of girl you marry, if you know what I'm saying. I mean, that's what I'm told by *some* people."

She flicked her eyes toward Broch.

Sean grimaced. "I am *not* getting involved in whatever this is."

Catriona sighed. "I'm sorry. I just wanted to confirm with

you that it is *totally* normal and common for couples to share a bed before marriage and such action doesn't mean the woman is a hoo-er."

Luther peered at Broch over his reading glasses and offered a low whistle "Boy, you'd better watch yourself because you're gonna *lose* this fight."

Sean nodded slowly. "Right on both accounts."

Broch crossed his beefy arms across his chest, staring in icy silence at the wall opposite him.

Catriona smiled. "Cool. I'm glad we got that settled. Please continue."

Sean sighed. "Great. Thanks. Go ahead, Luther."

Luther once again lowered his paper. "That's all I got. There's nothing to say Colin did it—"

"Except the body they found under his house," interjected Catriona.

"Right. That part's bad."

Sean leaned back in his chair. "Did you know a body decomposes faster if it hasn't bled out?"

"If it hasn't—" Catriona took a second and then closed her eyes. "The *expanding foam*. Whoever killed her was sealing the wound to speed up decomposition?"

Sean smiled. "You didn't figure that one out?"

She sneered. "You mentioned the foam on the phone and then ran away. I didn't know it was a *test*."

"Fail."

She stuck her tongue out at him.

He chuckled. "Anyway, it's a theory. The killer might have stopped the bleeding to be sure the body was found sooner."

"And Colin would be arrested sooner," mumbled Catriona.

Sean nodded. "Maybe. As for Timmy, I just heard from his sister. On the upside, the dancer he attacked is going to live.

She's very lucky."

"So is he," muttered Luther.

Sean nodded in agreement. "Timmy's blood tested positive for bath salts, which he swears he's never taken, so the next order of business is to find out how that happened."

Catriona remembered a news story about a man on a drug known as 'bath salts' who tried to rip off someone's face. Timmy's violence made more sense if he were on such a drug.

"Are we sure he didn't take them? From what I hear, he's not an angel when it comes to drugs."

"He *swears* he's never touched them. I asked around and no one remembers him ever having an interest in designer stuff. Coke, weed, maybe some ecstasy—but that's about it. And for all his faults, he's always been a professional when on set."

"Except when it comes to women," added Catriona. She'd heard rumors about Timmy's wild sex parties.

Luther chuckled. "I thought he fancied men when he started here. Then I found out that boy pulls down more—" He glanced at Catriona and cleared his throat. "I'm just sayin', he sure loves the ladies."

"Sex parties are a long way away from ripping out someone's throat," said Sean.

Catriona put a foot up on the edge of Sean's desk. "So you're thinking someone set him up too? Someone's after the studio?"

"It's a possibility." Sean poked Catriona's toe with his pen and she dropped her foot back to the ground.

"Who would have access to Colin *and* Timmy?"

"That's a good question."

"Could thay hae something in common? Someone wha hates thaim both fur an identical reason?"

All eyes turned to Broch and he scowled, appearing exasperated. "Fowk murdered fowk in mah time tae. Ah'm not glaikit. Ah hae the identical brains as ye dae."

Catriona looked at Sean. "Glay-kit?"

"*Stupid*. He's not stupid just because he's new to our time," translated Sean.

Hearing Sean admit to Broch's time-traveling past out loud, Catriona's gaze shot to Luther.

The big man chuckled. "I know all about your time-travelin' boyfriend. I met your pop, remember?"

Catriona nodded. She'd forgotten Luther had discovered Sean after his time jump. There'd been no reason to keep Broch's secret from him.

Sean looked at Broch. "You're right, son. I apologize if it seemed we were excluding you. You're part of the team now."

Broch nodded. "Aye. Thank ye."

"And you have a good point—we should check into anything the two of them have in common, in case this isn't about the studio, but about those two. Teena's death threat could be the usual overzealous fan stuff."

"I don't think the two of them could be any different," said Catriona, picturing Colin, the strapping action hero, standing beside the petite retired dancer.

"That's for sure," agreed Luther.

Broch sniffed. "Wummin."

"What?" asked Sean.

"Wummin. Ye said Timmy lik'd the lassies and Colin wis sleepin' with wummin he wisnae marry'n."

Catriona rolled her eyes. "I only said that to make a point with you."

"Ah ken. It remains true."

Sean sat forward in his chair. "Something to consider. Luther, why don't you see if you can get a list of people they've dated in the last year or two?"

Luther stood, grunting as his knees cracked. "I'll take a whole notebook."

Catriona stood as well. "I think I'm going to sniff around Timmy's dressing room. See if anything sets off any alarm bells."

"What about that video footage?" asked Luther.

She grimaced and Luther patted her shoulder. "I gotta guard who can finish up. Don't you worry, princess."

She grinned. "Thank you, Luther."

"Uh-huh."

Catriona looked at Broch. "You want to come to Timmy's with me?"

"Aye." He stood and they said their goodbyes.

In the hall, Broch elbowed Catriona. "Whyfer did Sean think *ye'd* be mad aboot Colin's new mistress?"

Catriona shook her head. "Don't even go there."

They walked in silence for a few more steps before Broch spoke again.

"Surely Colin cannae dance lik' me?"

Catriona giggled.

CHAPTER SIXTEEN

Catriona and Broch walked from Sean's office to the studio of *Ballroom Bounce.* Catriona ducked under the police tape crisscrossing the door to flip on the lights, which burst to life in a series of loud pops.

The large studio had been split into two sections: the area where filming took place, boasting a stage and the audience seats, and the back, housing rehearsal spaces, costume storage, and dressing rooms.

"They dance in 'ere?" asked Broch.

Catriona nodded. "It's a contest. People dance and then the judges, like Timmy, vote on who's the best. The losers go home. And of course, there's an audience sitting here that oohs and aahs at everything."

"And this is something ah cuid watch oan the television?"

"Yep. We film it here and then it shows up on your television, like *Magic Mike*."

Broch grunted. "That picture wis full of *lies*."

Catriona headed for the dressing room featuring Timmy's name on the door, happy to find that the doorknob turned without resistance.

The lights had been left on, illuminating a back wall

featuring an enormous mirror with a countertop and seating below it. The room was neat, with several rows of beauty products and makeup jars lining the counter, labels facing forward. A large bouquet of white gladioli sat in the corner on an enormous cement stand. Timmy expected flowers to arrive regularly.

On the wall to the left of the makeup area hung a dozen framed photos of Timmy dancing at different venues, as well as a smattering of plaques commemorating wins. He stood in most photos with hands held out in flourish, his trim, wiry body displayed in various stages of undress and wrapped in multiple colors of spandex.

Catriona opened and closed a row of three drawers running beneath the makeup bench. She found a few more half-filled cans of base makeup, nail clippers, and other personal hygiene items. Nothing that looked like bath salts.

"I don't know what I'm looking for," she said, sliding the last drawer shut. "It doesn't look like he does much in here except get pretty. I don't see any snacks that might have been tampered with. He doesn't keep food here."

"Whit dae bath salts keek lik'?"

"Like a bunch of little crystals. Like big salt or little crumbly stone."

Broch's gaze locked on a photo featuring Timmy in heavy clown makeup, wearing a revealing, sparkly outfit. He reached for the photo.

"Wis he eatin' them whin he wore this?" he asked, pulling the photo from the wall. As he did, a folded piece of paper fell from behind the photo to the ground.

Catriona stooped to grab the pink, lined paper and unfolded it. It looked as if it had been torn from a small book, as tall and wide as her outstretched palm. Loopy writing filled each line on one side. The bottom of the page also had a torn edge, as if someone had stripped off a hunk.

The contents started in the middle of a sentence rather than with a date, but the first-person account read like a diary entry.

She read aloud:

"T had the balls to sit there, not saying a word. It was humiliating. When I tried to get him to talk he laughed and told me it had all been fun and I needed to let it go. When I told him that wasn't how I saw it, he said too bad. He—"

She flipped over the page to find it blank but for tiny lettering along the tear line.

See how you like it.

"It stops there."

"Dae ye think it's important?"

"Could be. It could have been planted by the person who dosed him."

Broch flipped up the other frames, inspecting the backs and shaking them as best he could without removing them. Nothing else fell.

Catriona studied the photo Broch had removed. "Let's take this with us. Maybe it's special."

"Kin we ask Timmy if he kens aboot the note?"

She nodded. "Good idea. We need to go talk to Timmy."

Back in the studio parking lot, Catriona pulled two baggies from the back of her Jeep and slipped the letter inside one and the small frame inside the other, hoping the police could pull fingerprints from one or both.

After she was done with them, of course.

They drove to the hospital where Timmy sat handcuffed to a bed, eyes downcast and lip pouted, recovering from his self-inflicted wounds.

The dance judge's eyes sparked to life upon spotting Catriona in the hall, but an officer sitting outside the room rose from his chair to stop their progress. After a call to Sean for the obligatory string-pulling, they were admitted to Timmy's room for a quick visit.

"Oh Cat," said Timmy as she entered, his wrist jerking against his cuffs. "Look what they did to my beautiful smile."

He raised his upper lip, displaying the gap where his front tooth once stood.

Catriona stole a glance at Broch.

The Highlander kept his mouth shut.

"Hi, Timmy." She lay a hand on his.

"No touching," barked the officer from the hallway.

"Sorry."

Timmy gawked at Broch. "Why do you look familiar?"

Catriona sighed.

"He's the one who stopped you—"

Timmy's eyes grew wide. "*You* knocked out my *tooth*."

Broch grimaced. "Aye. Sorry."

Timmy waved a hand at him. "No, no. You did what you had to do. Did I hurt *you*?"

Broch shook his head. "Ye fought lik' a lynx."

Timmy flopped his head back into his pillow. "I'm so sorry. You know I'd never do anything like this if I were in my right brain. I don't have a violent bone in my body. It was the drugs. I don't know how—"

"I know. That's why we came to talk to you." Catriona nodded to Broch and he held out the framed photo.

"That's from my dressing room," said Timmy.

"Right. This fell out from behind it. Do you recognize it?"

She handed him the bagged letter.

Timmy took it with his uncuffed hand.

"Can you put my glasses on?" he asked.

Catriona spotted a pair of reading glasses on the table beside her and placed them on Timmy's face. She'd never noticed the freckles on his nose and cheeks before, but then again, she'd seen how much makeup he kept in his dressing room.

Timmy's scowl deepened as he read. "I don't understand. What is this?"

"I don't know. It looks like a diary entry about you."

"You think this is about *me*?"

"You don't? It refers to the person she's mad at as *T*."

"How do you know it's a she?"

Catriona shrugged. "Just guessing from the pink paper and flouncy handwriting."

He scoffed. "You *clearly* haven't spent much time around male dancers."

"It sounds to me like you jilted someone. Someone who thought his or her relationship with you was deeper than you imagined."

He handed the bag back to Catriona. "Doesn't ring any bells. Anyhow, I already gave Talia a list of everyone I work with or remember seeing naked in the last year. Luther asked her to get it from me."

Catriona turned the bag around to point at the torn edge. "Here it says *See how you like it.* Does that make any sense to you? Did you dose someone? Even as a joke maybe?"

Timmy shook his head and turned his face to the side, pressing it into the pillow.

"How could this happen to me?" he moaned.

Catriona didn't miss his evasive lack of an answer.

"The girl you attacked is going to live," she said.

He whipped his head back to face her. "For certain? She's out of the woods?"

She nodded. "Apparently. In case you were wondering."

"Of course, I was wondering. Talia told me there was

hope but...oh thank *God*. So they can't arrest me for murder?"

"No. *Attempted* murder is on the table, though."

He closed his eyes as if pained. "That's not good."

"No. So it would behoove you to think about this note. Could it be from someone you spent time with?"

His eyes began to tear. "I don't know. Can you leave it with me?"

"No. I can take a photo of it for you, but I need to turn it over to the police. It might help them prove someone dosed you."

Timmy grimaced. "Someone *did*. You know I'm always professional."

"Uh-huh."

"It's true. And bath salts? Why would I take that trash drug? I've got a bag of molly back at the house. I've got five eight-balls of coke—" He gasped and grabbed her wrist, his voice dropping to a whisper. "Oh my god. *I have those drugs at my house.* If they find those, they'll never believe I didn't take bath salts."

Catriona glanced toward the officer and whispered in Timmy's ear. "Tell me where. I'll see what I can do."

"In my underwear drawer. Oh, you're an *angel*."

She straightened. "Uh-huh. You should have mentioned this earlier."

Timmy wailed. "I can't *stand* this. Why would anyone do this to me?"

"I can't imagine."

He grabbed her hand. "Hurry. There's a key to my place under the potted cactus on the back porch."

She nodded and motioned to Broch to go.

"Sorry aboot yer tooth," he said, shuffling toward the door.

Timmy reached toward him with his free hand as they left.

"I forgive you."

Chapter Seventeen

Catriona and Broch drove to Timmy's mid-century modern masterpiece and parked on the circular drive curving in front of the low, square building. Large glass windows lined the front wall of the home, but for the spot in the center where a perky salmon-colored door screamed for attention.

Catriona jogged around the back of the house and spotted a cactus in an oversized pot. She tilted it back to find the key and a tiny folded piece of pink paper, no larger than a dime.

Why do I think that's not supposed to be there?

Gingerly pinching the edges, she unfolded the paper.

"Anither wee note?" asked Broch, appearing at her elbow.

She nodded.

"It's torn at the top and left side. I'm sure this fits at the bottom of the page we found earlier."

On one side of the otherwise blank paper, printed in small capitals, someone had written *IT HAPPENED HERE.*

"I think this confirms the note was planted by someone involved."

Catriona stared at the key. She hated to mess with it when the person who dosed Timmy had likely touched it, but if the police found a cache of drugs in Timmy's bedroom, no one would ever believe he was innocent.

As cavalier as his private life appeared, she believed he'd taken the bath salts. Not only did the diary entry appear to be proof someone was angry with him, but the disdain with which he'd referenced the drugs had convinced her he felt they were beneath him.

She pulled two pairs of latex gloves from her pocket and handed one pair to Broch.

"Put these on so we don't leave fingerprints everywhere."

Broch took a pair and wrestled to wrap his enormous paws with them.

She gathered the key and unlocked the door to Timmy's home. Entering the kitchen, she opened a few drawers until she found sandwich bags, into which she dropped the key and the tiny torn note.

She scanned the room. It seemed like a normal kitchen in the usual state of mess, and not one the police had already tossed.

"Doesn't look like the cops are in a hurry to prove Timmy was drugged. They haven't been here yet."

She heard a clicking noise and turned to find Broch turning on and off the gas stove burners.

"Ah lik' this muckle better than the flat heat we hae back at the apartment."

"We have electric."

"Ah lik' the fire."

"Yeah, well, I like mansions but I live in the apartment next to yours."

Catriona headed into the living room and down a hallway featuring the front-of-house glass on the left and a large mural of a dancing couple on the right. She skipped past a bathroom and two spare rooms to arrive in Timmy's bedroom.

The walls of Timmy's love shack were adorned with highly erotic photos of beautiful women, their naked bodies wet and bound to various black geometric shapes. Catriona was trying to calculate the impossible angle to which one woman had her leg raised when Broch wandered into the room. He gaped and looked at Catriona with an expression she could only describe as panic. It was as if he wanted to scoop her up and cart her out of the room.

"It's *art*," she offered.

He looked at the floor and rubbed his forehead.

"Och, 'tis *something*."

Catriona smiled. "Are you *blushing*?"

He shot her a look without raising his face.

She chuckled. "Big scary man with such delicate sensibilities."

The wall behind the bed boasted what looked like a series of padded black leather boxes, the bed itself draped by a plush, leather-trimmed blanket. Pillows wrapped in black sheets piled high at the head and a small doll wearing a tiny cowboy hat sat in the center of them staring forward with big brown eyes.

Catriona shuddered to think about what that doll had seen.

Dark purple cloth covered the remaining walls, and the master bath spilled into the room with only a glass wall separating the shower from the bedroom. Feasibly, someone could lie in bed and watch someone—or some*ones*—shower.

Catriona's lip reflexively curled. "This place makes me *want* to take a shower. Anywhere but *here*."

She jerked open a few bureau drawers, wincing with each pull for fear of what she might discover. After a mass of socks and undershirts, she unveiled a drawer stuffed with boxer briefs and *briefer* briefs. Bracing herself, she pushed a hand through the neatly folded piles until her fingers felt what turned out to be a gallon-sized resealable bag filled with drugs.

She held it up for Broch to see. "Got it."

"Guid. Let's gae."

She took a moment to scan the room. "*It happened here*," she mumbled. If the person who left the pink note had more room to be specific, she felt confident they would have singled out Timmy's bedroom as the exact place 'it' happened. From her angle beside the bed, she saw leather straps hanging from an eyebolt screwed into the wall between the puffy leather squares. She tugged on one strap to find handcuffs dangling from the end.

"Yikes. I guess Timmy's more at home being cuffed than I imagined."

Broch grunted his disapproval. "'Tis lik' a dungeon. Did he haud someone captive 'ere?'

"I dunno. I'm assuming it's a sex thing."

"A sex thing?"

"People tie each other up and have sex."

Broch scowled. "Tae keep them in the kip?"

"More or less."

They made their way back down the hall and into the kitchen. Broch stopped Catriona as she reached to open the back door, leaning close to whisper in her ear.

"Ah'd ne'er hae tae bind ye tae mah kip. Ye'd never want tae leave." He slid his hand down her arm, the trill of his finger on her skin quickening her breath.

Catriona's body felt like a piano wire stretched tight, begging to be played, but she resisted surrendering to his seduction. His uncharacteristically saucy comment was *clearly* another ploy to inch her toward accepting his proposal. The game was afoot.

"I can resist your charms all day, every day," she said.

He smiled. "Me tae. Ah kin dae *many* things *all day*."

She arched an eyebrow.

"Can you *not* touch me all day?"

"Aye. If ye willnae say yes to my proposal."

"Even if I do this?" She reached up and slid her fingers an inch into the top of his jeans.

"Och," he jumped away, clapping his arms across his chest several times as if he didn't know what to do with his hands.

He blushed a fiery red.

"Ye might hae tae tie me in they chains after all," he muttered.

She chuckled and felt for her phone with one hand while opening the backdoor with the other. She needed fresh air and something to distract her.

"You're going to lose this one, Kilty," she sang, stepping onto the porch.

"We'll see."

Catriona dialed Timmy's sister.

"Tell your brother we took care of his little problem. He'll know what I mean."

"I'm here with him now," said Talia.

Catriona heard Talia relay her message to Timmy. A moment later she heard his voice.

"Thank you so much, Cat. Feel free to keep whatever's in the bag for yourself."

She chuckled. "No thanks. Unless they're for treating venereal diseases because I might have caught four just *walking* into your bedroom."

Timmy laughed. "Girl, you're too funny."

"Listen, we found another note under the cactus with your key."

"You *did*? What did it say?"

"It was a sliver of paper. It said *it happened here*. Any chance this all has something to do with your little sex dungeon?"

Timmy huffed. "It shouldn't. Everyone who walks in there knows what they're doing. We're all adults." He paused.

"Though, it *happens.*"

"What happens?"

"The occasional misunderstanding. There's drinking, there are drugs, sometimes there are masks... The cast is ever-changing. That's what makes it *exciting.*"

Catriona frowned. "Let me ask you this. Do you know if you've ever dated any of the same women as Colin Layne?"

"It isn't out of the realm of possibility, but I don't recall anyone ever *mentioning* it. People don't talk about other lovers when they're with *me.* They forget them."

Catriona stuck out her tongue, pantomiming a gag.

"Did you eat anything at the house before you came into work today?"

"Just my coffee. I can't function without it."

"Made it yourself? Poured in the water, the whole deal?"

"Yes. Why?"

"Because the note was *with your key.* Whoever wrote it had access to your house. I just realized they could have put the bath salts in your coffee maker."

"Oooh..."

Catriona sighed. "Timmy, if you get out of this mess without prison time, you're going to have to slow your roll. No more parties."

"Catriona, if you get me out of this I'll never sleep with anyone again."

"Right. I won't hold my breath on that one."

Timmy giggled.

"I wouldn't either."

CHAPTER EIGHTEEN

Catriona drove back to Parasol at exactly the speed limit. The last thing she needed was to be pulled over with Timmy's Bag o' Fun in her trunk.

They returned to Sean's office to find him on the phone. She plopped the giant bag of drugs on his desk.

Sean scowled. "Perfect. Hey, can I call you back? Something just came up." He hung up and looked from the bag to Catriona. "Why does that look like a bag of drugs?"

"Pulled it out of Timmy's underwear drawer. Have you been to his house?"

Sean shook his head.

"It's pretty much a non-stop sex party over there at Casa Timmy. My guess is someone didn't like the experience and they're setting him up."

"Why do you say that?"

"The explicit artwork, the leather straps bolted to the wall behind the bed, the peek-a-boo shower... It's fifty shades of Timmy Grey. If a woman is doing this to him—and we have reason to believe so—no one who sees his bedroom is *ever* going to believe he's innocent of whatever she says he did."

"You think a woman dosed him?"

Catriona produced the baggies with the pink notes in them. "Big one fell out from behind a frame in his dressing room. The little one was under his cactus pot with his house key."

"They're *pink*," he said.

"That's one of the reasons I'm thinking it's a girl—"

"It's more than that. I was just talking to my contact at the coroner's office. They found a pink piece of paper under the spray foam in Cari's skull."

Catriona gasped. "Oh my God. How is this getting even more grisly? What did it say?"

"It wasn't readable. You can imagine..."

"I'd rather not."

Sean pulled at his chin. "So the papers tie the two cases together. You didn't happen to see a doll at Timmy's?

Catriona perked. "We did. What kind?"

"Cowgirl? Small. Marks near the mouth?"

"Och," said Broch.

Catriona nodded. "There was a doll like that in Timmy's bedroom, but I'd chalked it up as more of his weird sex paraphernalia. *Damn.* I should have grabbed that thing."

Sean grimaced. "So we have pink paper and a cowgirl doll to connect Timmy with Colin." He took a moment to read the notes. "Our mystery woman had access to both places? Timmy's dressing room and his house?"

"I guess so. I asked, and he only had coffee this morning. I'd get the police to start by testing his coffee machine for drugs."

"Good idea. I'll get the cops on it and make sure someone knows to bag the doll. Oh, and I've got the list of people who've dated or been in contact with Colin or Timmy." Sean slid a piece of paper across the desk and turned it so Catriona and Broch could read it. "There was one match on the lists."

The sheet had two columns on it, each with a list of

names. One name was circled on each.

"Jessie Walker?"

Sean nodded. Makeup artist. She worked on Colin, Timmy and *Teena*—though I don't know if her death threat is related yet."

"Do you have an address? We'll go check it out and look for a tie-in."

He handed her a printed photo of a petite, dark-haired young woman and another slip of paper with an address scrawled on it in Luther's handwriting.

Catriona took it, her head shaking. "He could have texted it to you."

"Why would Luther text when he has a perfectly good pen?"

Catriona wasn't sure if he was kidding or not.

Sean turned to Broch. "How are you doing? How's the pain?"

Broch lifted his arm. "'Tis fine. Wee stiff."

"That's what Pete said," mumbled Catriona.

Brochan snatched the address from Catriona's fingers. "We'll gae check on the lassie for ye."

He strode out the door.

Catriona shrugged at Sean. "Sensitive."

Sean shook his head. "You two, play nice."

Catriona jogged after Broch.

"Hey, you driving now?" she called after his retreating form.

"Pretend to be my husband," said Catriona as she knocked on Jessie Walker's second-floor apartment door.

Broch opened his mouth as if to protest as a petite blonde answered the door.

Catriona smiled. "Hi, we were looking for Jessie?"

"She's not here. I'm her roommate, Sandy." Smiling, the girl's gaze locked on Broch. "Are you an actor? Are you here for makeup?"

Broch grinned back. "Na."

Sandy tilted her head down, peering at him through her false lashes like a coy courtesan. "You *look* like an actor."

Catriona cleared her throat to break the spell. "Jessie isn't here?"

The girl snapped from her trance. "Huh? Oh. No. I haven't seen her in weeks."

"Weeks? You don't know where she went?"

"No. It's been nice, to be honest." The girl giggled. "I'm sorry. I didn't mean that *mean*...I meant, like, having the place to myself. Did you have an appointment with her or something?"

"No, I'm her sister. This is my husband, Bob Johnson."

Sandy flashed Broch a smile.

"Ah'm Bob," he echoed.

Sandy put her hand on her hip. "I didn't know Jessie had a sister. Nice to meet you. Do you want to come in?"

Catriona nodded. "Maybe for a second. Come on, Bob."

Scowling, Broch followed her inside.

Sandy shut the door and leaned her back against it, looking around the apartment as if she were lost as to what to do next.

"You want something to drink?" she asked.

Catriona shook her head. "Oh, no, we're good. Would you mind if we looked in Jessie's room? We haven't heard from her and I'm worried."

"You can't. I mean, you *could*, except she locks her room."

"She has a key lock on her bedroom door?"

"She's kind of..."

As Sandy twisted, searching for the words, Catriona realized the two girls didn't have the most idyllic roommate relationship. Sandy was afraid of offending Jessie's 'sister' with too much honesty.

Catriona raised a hand. "Don't be afraid of offending me. Jessie has always been *odd*." She pulled her unflattering description of Jessie from the air, hoping her guess would hit the mark.

Sandy nodded enthusiastically, eyes squinting. "She is, *right*?"

"Yes. Always has been. So please, tell me anything you know that might help us find her."

Sandy nodded. "Well, when she first moved in I thought she was shy, but over the last few months she's been getting...*weird*."

"Weird, how?"

"She started locking her door, staying out late. Sometimes not coming home at all."

"Sounds like she has a boyfriend?"

"That's what I thought at first, but the makeup thing—is that something she did at home?"

"She always wanted to be a makeup artist."

"No, I know that's her job, but the last few weeks she was going to work with...you know." Sandy drew a circle in the air around her face with her index finger.

Catriona's brow knit. "I don't understand?"

Sandy grimaced. "Sorry. I thought maybe it was something she always did. She's been making up her face up like a *doll*, but like, a *creepy* doll. Maybe it was for work?"

"She went to work made-up like a doll?"

"I only caught her on her way out like that twice but, I dunno. She's definitely been acting *super* weird the last few weeks."

"Parasol Pictures fired her three weeks ago," said Catriona.

Sandy's jaw dropped.

"Oh. *Wow*. Where was she going then? She's been leaving the same time she always left for work..." The girl tilted back her head to stare at the ceiling. "She must have got another job?"

"Maybe. Any idea where?"

Sandy shrugged. "She works on movies, right? The doll stuff was probably make-up for whatever she was working on. She probably tried it on herself?"

"Maybe it was her version of a resume?"

Sandy pointed. "Yeah, maybe."

Catriona nodded, but she couldn't think of anything they'd filmed at Parasol in the last month featuring creepy dolls. Jessie might have been auditioning for jobs elsewhere.

"Ah'm guan tae hae a keek in her room," said Broch.

The girl's expression scrunched like a balled piece of paper and she gawked at Broch as if he'd spoken in another language. Which, Catriona had to admit, he sort of had.

The girl fell into nervous giggles. "Like I said, I don't mind, but she locks it so—"

Broch looked at Catriona and motioned to the back of the living room with his eyes.

"Hey, Sandy, come and look at this." Catriona walked toward the windows overlooking the street and motioned to the girl to follow her. With a last glance at Broch, Sandy followed and the two peered through the windows together.

Catriona pointed to the street. "I thought I saw Jessie's car out here. What kind of car does she have now?"

"An old red one. Though I saw her in a blue truck before she left, though. It looked about a million years old."

"Ford? Chevy?"

Sandy shrugged.

Behind her, Catriona heard a pop.

"Okay. Thanks." She called out for Broch. "Hey honey, where'd you go?"

"Ah'm in 'ere."

They followed Broch's voice into Jessie's room.

Broch stood inside, staring at them.

He shrugged.

"Door wis open."

Catriona spotted the splintered wood around the door jamb and glanced at Sandy to see if she'd noticed.

The girl was too busy ogling Broch, twirling her long brown hair around a finger.

No reason to worry she'd notice the door.

"You talk funny. Where are you from?" Sandy asked him.

Catriona looked away, rolling her eyes for Broch to see. He remained guileless and grinning.

"Ah'm fae Scootlund, lassie," he purred.

The girl giggled. "That accent is *amazing*."

"Thank ye."

"*Ah'm fae Scootlund lassie*," mocked Catriona under her breath. She pushed past the Highlander and stopped, staring at the corner of the room.

Someone had erected a shrine. There were photos, some of Jessie now, and some that looked like they could be her as a girl. Ribbons, candles, bits of jewelry, several dolls, and a ceramic horse rounded out the collection.

Besides the shrine, a pile of small dolls lay jumbled on top of one another, each dressed in a cowgirl outfit, tiny cowboy hats pinned to their heads.

Above the shrine in shaky red scrawl it read, *I will avenge you sweet girl.*

Catriona pressed her finger against the lettering and glanced at her fingertip.

So heavy-handed I thought it might be blood.

She glanced up to find no one paying attention to her or the shrine. Broch remained in the doorway, blocking Sandy's view of the shattered door lock, chatting with the girl. Catriona heard her giddy tittering.

Sandy looked as if she'd twist herself into a knot of ecstasy if Broch said one more guttural word.

"Sandy, can you look at something for me?" called Catriona.

The girl slid past Broch, not trying with any real effort to avoid rubbing against him as she did.

For crying out loud...

Catriona pointed to the shrine.

"Was this always here?"

The smile fell from Sandy's face as she wondered at the shrine.

"*No.* That's like, *cray.*"

"Is it possible someone was able to get into this room?"

"You think someone else made that? Not her?"

Catriona pointed to the red words on the wall. "It looks like a shrine dedicated *to* her."

Sandy stared at the lettering and shivered. "Ooh. That's creepy."

"Could someone have gotten in here?"

Sandy fell silent and appeared to ponder the possibilities. "I mean, I'm not here *all* the time. I'm an actress, but I waitress at night."

Catriona smiled.

Of course you do.

"Maybe she gave someone a key? Her parents? Uh, I mean *our* parents?"

Sandy frowned. "I thought she said your mom's dead or gone or something? She mentioned her dad once or twice..."

"Right. She would. Mom's flaky to say the least." Catriona laughed to distract Sandy from her floundering lies.

The girl took another step forward, studying the collection of memorabilia, her face twisted with concern.

"That's what she looked like," she said, pointing to the dolls.

"Who? Jessie?"

Sandy nodded. "She was dressed like *they* are. Just like that. But her face was—*worse*."

"Do you have any current photos of her?"

"No—oh, there's some on Facebook?"

Catriona made a mental note to tell people she was a distant cousin in the future. Certainly, Jessie's sister would know she was on Facebook. "Right. I, uh, don't use social media. She has a Facebook account?"

Sandy looked at Catriona as if she'd grown a glittering unicorn horn. "*Yeah.*"

"Can you look up her page for me and let me know the last time she posted?"

"Sure. Let me grab my phone."

Sandy bopped out of the room.

"Whit dae ye think?" asked Broch when she'd gone.

"I think she's too young for you."

"Ah wisnae flirting wi' her."

Catriona squinted one eye and invoked Broch's accent. "Ah'm fae Scootlund, little lassie..."

He smirked. "Ah dinnae sound lik that."

Sandy reentered the room, staring at her phone. "It looks like she hasn't posted anything in like three weeks."

"How about before that? Did she post often?"

"Every other day or so. She'd post pictures of her makeup jobs and stuff. This is the last one she did."

Sandy held up the phone and Catriona glanced at the image of a familiar smiling woman.

Fiona Duffy.

The tight scarf she wore around her throat in the photo

identified the production as *Camping Under the Stars*. Catriona had seen the commercials for it and all the actors had worn similar color-coded ties.

"*This* woman was her last client?"

Sandy nodded.

"Show him."

Sandy pointed the phone at Broch and his eyes widened. "Na..."

"You guys know her?"

Catriona grunted.

Oh sure. She's my sister who time-traveled here to make my life miserable.

"Could I find Jessie's Facebook page by searching her name?"

"Yeah. That's how I found it. I didn't have it saved or anything."

"Great. Thank you. Look. I'm not entirely sure what's going on yet but there's a chance I'm going to have to call the police and have them look at this. Can you not touch anything until I get back to you?"

The girl shrugged. "She pays rent three months in advance so I wouldn't try to move her out for another month and a half anyways."

"Great. Thank you. Let's leave the door shut? Don't touch anything. The police will want to check for fingerprints."

"No problem." Sandy frowned. "Is it okay if I get the front door lock changed? This is all kind of creepy..."

"Sure. Of course."

As they left the room, Catriona noticed a small piece of paper tucked between Sandy's fingers. They said their goodbyes and she watched as the girl covered Broch's hand with her opposite hand while shaking goodbye with him. When she removed her hand, the paper was gone and Broch glanced at his closed fist.

Catriona scowled.

That little hussy...

They headed for the Jeep and Sandy stood in her doorway, waving until the elevator doors closed.

"Ah dinnae lik' the leuk of that shrine," said Broch as they stepped outside.

Catriona sighed. "It looks like someone knows she's dead."

"Aye. Felt that way."

Catriona glanced down. Kilty's hand was still closed.

"She gave you her phone number, didn't she?"

Broch unfurled the paper and sniffed it. "It smells pretty."

"I bet." Catriona chuckled. "You know you're not going to trick me into marrying you by flirting with other people, right?"

He smirked and made a show of stuffing the paper in his pocket.

CHAPTER NINETEEN

Catriona peeped at Broch side-eyed as they rode the elevator together to their apartments.

His eyes were closed.

Poor thing. That wound is catching up with him.

The elevator stopped with a shudder and his lids sprung open. He rocked heel to toe to catch his balance and glanced at her to see if he'd been caught catnapping. Finding her staring, he bounced his pecs, one and then the next, grinning.

She arched an eyebrow. "You are *so* not allowed to watch stripper movies anymore."

"*Stripper*," he echoed, seeming to enjoy the sound of the word. "Ah'm going tae hae tae practice mah knee slide a wee bit mair."

"Your dancing might have actually *delayed* any chance of marriage for an additional year."

"Na."

"And you're not fooling me. You're falling asleep on your feet. You need a break."

He scowled. "Ah dae nae."

They stopped in front of her door.

"Whit noo?"

She frowned. "I'm serious. You should rest. How does your wound feel?"

"'Tis grand."

She spotted a small stain on his shirt. "Maybe I should look at it again. It's in a bad spot. Every time you move—it looks wet again."

"Aye. The shield fell aff in the shower. Ah forgot tae tell ye."

Catriona sighed. "You're going to have to be more careful. Do me a favor, go rest a little while?"

He frowned. "Whit are ye going to dae?"

"I have work on my computer to do."

Broch glanced at his door. "Aye. Ah'll tak' a wee nap. Bit tell me if we hae tae gang anywhere."

"I will, I promise."

He leaned down to kiss her on her hairline and she felt herself warm.

"Ye be careful," he murmured.

"What do you think can happen to me in my apartment?"

He shrugged. "Ah just worry about my bride when ah'm nae there to protect ye."

"Oh shut *up*." She laughed and smacked him on the hip as he twirled away and headed for his room, chuckling.

She watched him wink and disappear inside his apartment.

She waited a beat and then beelined for the elevator.

Catriona pulled her Jeep to the curb outside Fiona's house and took a deep breath. It couldn't be a coincidence Fiona Duffy was the last person Jessie Walker worked for before she went missing.

It couldn't.

Fiona was playing the long game, of that Catriona was certain. She didn't know why or what the woman hoped to accomplish, but she knew one thing—her *sister* was bad news.

Catriona walked down the walkway and knocked on the door. A figure moved on the opposite side of the Craftsman-style home's stained glass window and Catriona felt nerves writhing in her stomach like a ball of garden snakes. She hadn't brought a gun. Why did she feel like she needed one?

Stick to the case. Don't let her suck you into anything.

Catriona repeated the thought in her mind like a mantra. It seemed to her Fiona *liked* getting a rise out of her, and this time, she wasn't going to let it happen.

The door opened.

And you are...not Fiona.

A blonde woman at least ten years older than Fiona blinked at her.

"Can I help you?"

Catriona's mouth fell open and her planned speech caught in her throat.

"I, um, Fiona?"

"I'm sorry?"

"I was looking for Fiona Duffy? I thought, I mean, I dropped her off here..."

The woman smiled, her eyes squinty. "That's so *funny*. Some mail showed up for her today. That was kind of *exciting*. I loved her on *California Knights*."

Catriona let this information process long enough that the woman became curious why she was still standing on her doorstep.

"And you are?"

Catriona snapped from her thoughts. "Sorry. Catriona Phoenix. You?"

"Patricia Timms."

"Nice to meet you, Patricia. Do you mind if I ask how long you've lived here?"

"Ten years. Though we were in France for the last six months for my husband's work. The agency rented our place to Ms. Duffy while we were gone, but we never met her."

"Oh, do you know where she moved?"

"No. She didn't leave a forwarding address, but I guess famous people don't leave their addresses with just anybody." She laughed.

Catriona's shoulders slumped. She hadn't realized how much she was looking forward to talking to her supposed sister until the chance had passed. *Where had Fiona gone?* Maybe she'd returned to ancient *Scootlund.* That would be a good thing. Or maybe their father had come after all...

I'll get in touch with her agent. Do a little digging.

Fiona was a working actress, as far as she knew, so it wouldn't be too hard to track her down.

The blonde woman remained in the doorway, staring at her.

Catriona flashed a smile. "Sorry, lost my train of thought. Thanks. Sorry to bother you." She turned to return to her Jeep.

"Wait," called the woman. "Are you going to go to Fiona's new place? Are you a friend of hers?"

Catriona nodded.

Sure. Friend. Let's go with that.

The woman frowned, unconvinced, so Catriona added another layer of trust.

"I work for the studio."

Fiona didn't work for Parasol Pictures, but over the years Catriona had found saying *I work for the studio* encouraged star-struck people to trust her with almost any information. Nobody knew which actors worked for which studios.

As predicted, she watched the woman's eyes light up, her

mouth shaping into a little "O" of awe.

"Ooh, maybe you could give her the mail we received? I don't have any way to get it to her and I don't want her to think we're keeping it on purpose. Selling it on Ebay or something."

The woman tittered another nervous laugh.

The blonde disappeared inside and reappeared with several letters and a clothing catalog in her hand. She offered Catriona a sheepish grin. "It's all junk. She probably doesn't want it. But if you find her maybe you could let her know *I* gave it to you. If she wants to come by and let me know where to send anything else we get."

Catriona took the letters. "I'm sure she'll want to stop by and thank you personally. I'll let her know."

She'd do no such thing but the idea of it seemed to make the woman happy.

Patricia gasped. "Thank you. Tell her I loved her in *California Ice,* too," she said, invoking the name of a cheesy primetime soap opera about California hockey players' wives who ran a high-end jewelry boutique together. Fiona had played the bitchiest wife, from what Catriona could recall from the commercials.

Actors were generally typecast for a reason.

She grinned. "Will do."

Catriona returned to her vehicle and set the junk mail on the seat next to her. She called Parasol and told the new girl, Anne, someone might call her soon to confirm Catriona had a meeting with Fiona Duffy.

She needed Anne to back up her story.

"No problem," said Anne.

Catriona next called Hell Hound Pictures, Fiona's home studio, and in a frantic voice told the woman on the line she had a meeting at Fiona's home but had lost the address. She gave them Anne's number for confirmation, and after waiting on hold for a minute, the woman returned to rattle off Fiona's new address.

Nice job, New Girl.

Catriona hung up and stared at her steering wheel.

I know that address.

She knew exactly where Fiona lived. Los Angeles had recently started building high-rises, relying on modern advances in building technology and tossing concerns about earthquakes.

Fiona's high-rise apartment stood directly behind Parasol Pictures. Catriona could see the building from her window.

She growled.

Fiona couldn't have moved closer to her without moving into her *closet.*

Catriona slammed the Jeep into gear and flew to Fiona's new home. The high-rise loomed ahead of her, a swanky monstrosity of gleaming white walls and tinted windows. After she parked, a gray-haired doorman expedited the way for her, and by the time she announced her arrival to the lobby attendant, any trepidation she'd had about talking to Fiona had disappeared.

Nerves had been shoved aside by *fury.*

"Let me see if Ms. Duffy is available," said the man behind a Carrara marble desk, lifting an ornate phone that appeared swiped from an early "talkie" movie. "May I tell her who is calling and what this concerns?"

Catriona frowned. "You can tell her it's her sister and that it's none of your business."

The man tucked back his chin, pressing his lips tight with disapproval at her answer. He dialed, and a moment later Catriona heard a woman's muffled voice on the opposite end of the line.

"Your sister is here to see you," said the man. The way he said the word *sister* implied he didn't entirely believe the claim.

"Oh, yes. Very good, Ms. Duffy."

He hung up, settling the phone into its cradle as if it were made of china. "She said to come up. The elevator is behind you. You'll need this key." He handed her a plastic card. "Please return it to the desk when you're done. She's on the fifteenth floor, number fifteen hundred and one."

With a saccharine smile, Catriona took the card and rode to Fiona's floor, trying hard not to admire the wood veneer and gleaming gold trim of the elevator. For its ultra-modern exterior, the building's *interior* design invoked old Hollywood.

When the doors slid open, Fiona stood in the hallway, leaning against the wall with her pipe-cleaner arms folded across her chest, smiling.

"Fancy meeting you here, sis."

Catriona scowled and stepped into the hallway.

"Nice elevator."

"Thank you."

"Place is charming."

"I thought so."

Fiona wore impossibly tight, fashionably ripped jeans and a deep-scoop black t-shirt that appeared unremarkable in every way except she'd probably paid eight hundred dollars for it.

They didn't share the same body type. Fiona might have been telling the truth about Catriona taking after their mother and her favoring their father. Catriona wasn't sure she could fit her *arm* into the leg of Fiona's jeans.

She thrust forward the wad of mail given to her by Fiona's landlords. "The people from your rented house wanted you to have these."

Fiona took the mail and strolled toward her apartment as she shuffled through the pile. She pushed the door open with her foot and walked inside, leaving the door open behind her.

Catriona rolled her eyes. *Too much effort to ask me to follow? I'm supposed to waddle along behind her like a dog, I guess.*

She followed Fiona inside to find the old world charm stopped at the elevator. Fiona's white and gray modern décor led to a wall of glass overlooking the Parasol Pictures lot. Catriona scanned the view until she spotted her building. The light wasn't right in the late afternoon, but at night Fiona could see directly into her lit apartment. She was sure.

"That was one of the selling points," said Fiona, tossing the mail onto the long expanse of marble stretching across her kitchen island. "Views of Parasol Pictures' lot."

"Little cozy for an estranged family like ours, isn't it?"

Fiona shrugged. "*Aw.* I thought you'd be flattered."

Catriona swallowed, taking a moment to find her center. Fiona was already doing that *thing*—making her feel off-balance, teasing, ever implying she knew more about Catriona's life than *she* did. She felt like a wounded bird and Fiona, the cat, was eager to play.

She needed to shift the focus to something a little less on Fiona's turf.

"I'm here to ask you about Jessie Walker."

In a low whisper, Fiona repeated the name several times as she walked around her apartment, dragging her finger along chair backs as if deep in thought.

"Not ringing a bell."

"Makeup artist. She worked for Parasol but moonlighted. She was assigned to you when you filmed *Camping Under the Stars.*" Catriona found it hard not to groan as she said the name of the program. *Camping* pushed C-to-F-list actors on adventure excursions, where they fell in and out of various love triangles. The *Under the Stars* part was blatant sexual innuendo, though she didn't know which stars Fiona had found herself beneath.

"Oh, *Jessie*. Right. I never knew her last name."

"Understandable. You must have a lot on your mind. That's the kind of show where careers go to die, after all."

Ha! Take that. Nailed it.

Catriona tried not to smirk.

She hoped to find Fiona *reeling* from the blow of her caustic wit, but her sister only seemed to grow more amused.

"It pays the bills."

Catriona scanned the apartment.

Clearly.

Fiona continued. "My stint in jail has garnered me quite a bit of new interest. I might be writing a book about my ordeal."

"Fantastic. Tell me about Jessie."

Fiona shrugged. "What about her? She made me look dewy-fresh in the forest. That's all I needed her to do. What's your interest in her?"

Catriona considered how much she should share. "She's a person of interest in an investigation."

Fiona laughed. "You sound like a real cop. An investigation into what? Studio crimes? Tell me what happened."

Before Catriona could sort through what information she wanted to share, Fiona gasped.

"Timmy Grey? Is it that? Or, wait, no, the *murder*. Colin Layne and the girl under the house. Is she involved with that?"

Fiona's eyes sparkled with what looked like excitement—as if each of the tragedies were lava cakes with hidden fonts of chocolate oozing just for her.

"How do you know about all of that?" asked Catriona.

Fiona whistled. "I keep up with the news. Things have been hot at Parasol over the last twenty-four hours, haven't they?"

Catriona refused to rise to the bait. "Did Jessie ever

mention to you she was angry at anyone?"

Fiona shrugged. "No. I don't know that I ever said a word to her." She leaned against her sofa. "Is that what you came to ask me?"

Catriona glanced out the window at her apartment. "Yes. If that's all you have to say about Jessie. If I think of anything else I'll be sure to wave at you from my window."

Fiona grinned. "I'll be watching."

Catriona clenched her fists, digging her fingernails into her palms. She wanted to grab the smirking minx and *make* her answer her questions.

She needed to leave.

She turned and walked toward the door. Hand on the knob, she paused.

"You said our father would find us if we were near each other."

"Mm-hm."

Catriona turned. "Is that why you moved closer to me?"

Fiona smiled. "Now why would I *want* him to find us?"

Catriona gritted her teeth, but the words spat from her lips before she could stop them.

"Brochan remembers you, you know. He remembers telling you to leave him alone when your sorry ass tried to seduce him."

Catriona hadn't wanted to mention Broch, but she found it hard to regret it. For the first time, the smirk dropped from Fiona's face.

"There's more to that story." Fiona took a few steps forward, her body trembling with anger. "Tell him to think on *that* a little longer."

Fiona reached out and poked Catriona just above her left hip.

Catriona flinched and instinctively slapped away Fiona's hand.

The women glared at each other until Catriona peeled herself away.

"I'll catch up with you later, *Sis*," she growled.

Fiona responded with a mirthless smile of her own.

"I'll be here."

Catriona left, pulling the door behind her with a little more force than necessary.

The elevator's charms were lost to her on the way to the lobby. She slapped her key on the desk of the attendant, shocked the smug look from his face, and stormed toward the exit.

Catching the eye of the doorman, she slowed her roll and stopped to speak with him.

"Have you worked here long?" she asked.

"Since it opened last year," he said.

The man's gentle demeanor helped Catriona check her wrath. It wasn't fair of her to take her anger out on the old man. She took a deep inhale and let it out slowly before continuing.

"I have a question for you. I love my sister's place. She just bought fifteen-oh-one. Is there any trick to how I can get myself an apartment here? Do they ever come up for sale?'

The man shook his head, chuckling. "No, ma'am. She got lucky with that one, even if someone else didn't."

"What do you mean?"

"Gregory Pitkin lived there."

Catriona frowned. "Why does that name sound familiar?"

The man's voice dropped to a conspiratorial whisper. "He's the guy who shot up his ex-wife and then killed himself. She lived, thank God. His place went up for sale a week later."

"And Fiona jumped on it."

He chuckled. "She more than jumped on it. She'd already put in a bid."

Catriona scowled. "What do you mean? You mean she put

in a bid *before* he died?"

He nodded. "Craziest thing. She'd come in a week earlier and said she'd visited that apartment and wanted to buy it. Said if it ever came up, she'd be willing to pay—" He shuffled. "I shouldn't tell you what she paid for it, but it was more than they would have gotten on the market."

"So to get an apartment of my own here, all I have to do is guess who's going to die and throw too much money at it?"

The man laughed.

"That's   the   way   to   do   it."

CHAPTER TWENTY

Edinburgh, Scotland. 1833.

The rope tightened around Brochan's throat, jerking his body to an upright position. He fumbled for the noose, fingers digging into his flesh as he tried to pry it from his windpipe. A boot pressed the center of his back, ramming against his spine, his attacker using leverage to choke him. A second rope looped around his wrist, pulling his fingers away from his throat and behind his back. A hand grasped his opposite wrist and pulled it to join his other.

His arms were bound behind him as he gasped for air like a landed fish.

The noose loosened and the black spots clouding Brochan's vision cleared. Only then did he notice the figure in front of him.

A woman in men's leggings. She lit a lamp and smiled.

Fiona.

"I've been thinking about what you said during your visit to the forest the other day," she whispered, lowering to a squat to stare into his eyes. She maneuvered to his left to prevent him from kicking her.

Brochan tried to speak, but the rope tightened, choking his words into a raspy squawk.

A figure circled from behind him to stand near Fiona. Broch recognized Mathe and presumed he'd been the one to bind his hands. Judging by the size of the foot on his spine, he guessed Greer stood behind him, tugging the ends of the rope as if they were the reins of a runaway horse. He searched the shadows as best he could for the location of Harry, but could not find him. He guessed the chubby man had remained outside as a lookout.

Fiona ran her nails from Broch's temple to his chin, following the path of the scar there.

"I wonder who gave you this," she mumbled. She rested her fingers beneath his chin and stared into his eyes. "You said my sister died."

"Sister?" Broch croaked the word before Greer jerked on the rope to silence him once more.

"Yes. I'm *Fiona*. My father's favorite. It warmed my heart to hear he'd been calling Catriona by my name, but then, I took after his side of the family. Catriona favored Mama..." She leaned in to whisper in his ear. "She was more like you."

Mathe sneered and spat before commencing to wander the room, searching for anything of worth. He lifted a pot and several hooks fell from the rim, clattering to the floor.

Brochan's eyes darted to the left toward where his adoptive father slept in the back of the blacksmith shop. He didn't want the old man to wake. Gone were the days when the strapping man might have battled the three intruders on some equal footing. If they never knew of his presence, the better.

Luckily, in addition to growing weaker, the old man's hearing had dwindled. The rattling pothooks went unheard.

Fiona turned to glare at Mathe as he gathered the hooks, and Greer tugged at Brochan's noose, no doubt in fear he'd use the distraction as a window of opportunity to escape.

Mathe retreated to the corner of the room to lean against the wall as Fiona refocused on Brochan. She pressed her index finger to the middle of his forehead and traced down to the tip of his nose.

"While we were in the forest I realized *how* much like Catriona you are. I'd tried my best to sway you, but you resisted my charms. A common man wouldn't have been able to do that."

Fiona pulled a knife from a scabbard on her side. It was a strange and beautiful serpentine blade, the side edged with multiple ripples, as if it were a small, portable river, ending at a deadly point. Brochan couldn't help but think he'd like the chance to replicate it, should he live through the evening.

"You said Catriona died. I didn't think that was possible for our people. So I went to her lair and dug her up. I found her bones."

Brochan lunged against his bindings and Greer jerked back, but not before he swallowed a great gulp of air. He strained against the rope, inching forward until his nose nearly touched Fiona's. She didn't move. She smiled, seemingly amused by his anger.

Brochan felt the rope around his wrists loosen.

Mathe doesn't know how to tie a knot.

He worked at the rope to free his hands, continuing to strain against the noose to distract Greer.

Nearly there...

His gasp of oxygen expended, Brochan again saw stars. He ceased straining and leaned back, hoping to find enough air to keep from blacking out. Unable to speak, he glared at Fiona, projecting his anger as best he could.

"Ah'd hold still if ah wur ye," Greer whispered in his ear.

He smelled her sour breath and turned away his head.

Fiona reached out and pulled his chin back to face her.

"I saw Catriona dead, so I've come to visit you. You'll be

my experiment."

Without a moment of hesitation, Fiona thrust her curvy knife into Brochan's lower abdomen.

Broch felt the *pop* of his flesh give way to the point of her blade. Pain radiated from the wound into his chest and groin until his whole body felt aflame with agony.

He jerked back. The noose loosened and he sucked a ragged gasp of air.

Fiona glanced at Greer. "Release him. I need to finish this now."

The rope slipped from Brochan's neck and Greer's boot pushed him forward, shoving the blade deeper into his gut.

With a quick jerk, Fiona retracted the knife from his body. Brochan knew immediately she'd served him no kindness by doing so. As that river-shaped blade flowed from him, so did his life.

Fiona raised her arms into the air, the serpentine blade flashing in the lamplight.

As she poised to slice open his throat, Broch realized her intentions.

She wants tae see if ah kin die as Catriona did.

With what little strength remained in his body, Broch jerked his right arm and his hand slipped loose from his bindings. He reached up to grab Fiona's wrist, twisting the fragile joint as he pulled her across his legs.

She cried out and dropped the blade.

The rope that had been around his neck swept past Brochan's field of vision as Greer attempted to regain the hold she'd had on him. He caught the rope with his left hand and jerked it away, his opposite hand still holding Fiona's wrist as she writhed to free herself from his grasp.

Tossing the rope aside, he grabbed the hilt of the wicked knife now lying on the ground. Arcing it behind his head, he felt the blade bite flesh. Greer yelped, scrambling back and away from him.

On the opposite side of the room, Mathe came to life, grabbing something on a table beside him. Brochan kicked Fiona off of him, launching her into the air. She struck her head on a large metal pot as she landed and collapsed into a heap.

A renewed vigor pumping through his veins, Brochan jumped to his feet, roaring in pain as the knife wound in his lower abdomen demanded attention.

A bottle of Scotch struck the stone wall behind him and exploded, covering him in alcohol and peppering him with glass.

Broch and Mathe ran at each other. Broch connected a shattering blow to the man's jaw. Mathe spun away, bouncing against the wall.

With the knife still in his other hand, Broch stepped forward to finish Mathe.

A voice rang out behind him.

"Stop noo or ah'll kill him!"

Broch turned to find Greer standing over his adopted father. The old man knelt at her feet, his once-massive body withered and shaking. Greer held a plain, but no less deadly, knife to his throat.

It broke Brochan's heart to see the man felled by a scrawny dirt mouse.

Greer's left hand held the old man by his hair, her blade pressed at his throat. Her arm bled from where Brochan had caught her with Fiona's weapon.

Brochan considered stalling, hoping the loss of blood would drop Greer, but a glance at his wound told him time was not his friend. A steady ooze ran from his belly, soaking the great kilt he'd neglected to remove before falling into bed that night. He'd been drinking with Gavin. It was why he hadn't awoken until it was too late.

The room spun and Brochan fell to his knees, his burst of energy expended.

Less time than ah thought…

Still cradling his jaw, Mathe scrambled forward. Brochan raised his blade and made a weak swipe at the man, but Mathe easily avoided him to shake Fiona awake. She moaned as Mathe jerked her to her feet and dragged her past Greer toward the door.

They were nearly gone when Fiona's eyes sprang wide, her gaze locking on Brochan's. She lunged, reaching for the Highlander with both hands. Mathe's arms tightened around her waist, restraining her.

"No. Stop. I have to kill him," she said.

Mathe wrestled to keep her still. "Shut it. We hae to gae. He'll nae survive the wound."

She wailed. You don't understand, I have to kill him *dead*."

Mathe dragged Fiona from the room. Brochan's attention shifted to Greer, who offered him one last snarl. His father remained on his knees, eyes closed. Greer bolted away from him and out the door.

At first, Broch thought he'd imagined the motion of Greer's blade beneath his father's chin as she made her escape.

Then a thin line of red appeared on the old man's throat.

Time seemed to slow.

All at once, his father's hands flew to his throat, as if jerked by strings.

Blood spilled through his fingers.

"Na!" Broch fell forward from his place wobbling on his knees, reaching for his father.

Their eyes met for a moment and then the old man fell forward on his face, limp as a discarded marionette.

"Na…na…" Broch dragged himself a few inches across the stone floor, his extremities failing him. Breath growing more shallow with every inhale, his gaze locked on his father's wide, still eyes. His middle finger reached the old man's arm, and he used the tip of it to stroke the gray hair there, his eyelids growing heavy.

The last thing he heard was a final wail from Fiona, outside the blacksmith shop.

"I   need   to   kill   him   dead."

CHAPTER TWENTY-ONE

"Wake up. Ooh!"

Broch opened his eyes to find himself sitting up in bed. Catriona stood beside him, and he followed her wide-eyed gaze to find his fingers wrapped around her wrist. Embarrassed, he released his grip as if she were scalding.

"Ah'm sorry. Ah wis dreaming."

Catriona scowled, rubbing her wrist. "I know. I heard you screaming from next door. What happened?"

Broch recalled his dream and dropped his head into his hand. "Fiona."

"Again?"

"She killed my da."

"Sean? How is that—"

"Na, the man whit raised me after...after ah jumped tae the eighteen hundreds. After ye died."

"Right. That time I died." Catriona sat on the bed beside him. "Why would she kill your father?"

Broch took a deep breath and leaned his head against the wall behind his bed. "She came tae murdur *me*. Ah think she wanted tae see if she cuid. She didnae believe we cuid die lik' ye did."

"And by *we*, you mean time travelers?"

"Aye."

"But she killed your dad instead?"

"Nae exactly. She stabbed me and her friend wi' the mossy teeth cut mah da's throat."

He looked down at the scar on his belly. The wound had been ragged and bleeding when Catriona found him on the Parasol Pictures lot. Though it no longer bled, it didn't look *right*.

Catriona's attention also fell to his abdomen. "Is it me, or does that scar look redder than it did yesterday?"

Broch nodded. Even in the filtered light of the lot security lights peeping through his blinds, he could see the scar looked angrier than it had for some time.

"That's whaur she stabbed me."

Catriona gasped. "That's where she *poked* me."

"Whit?"

"She mentioned you and poked me *there*."

"When?"

"Um, I may have run out to ask her some questions while you were sleeping."

He scowled. "Ah tellt ye tae come git me if ye gaed anywhere."

"I know. I'm sorry. It was a spur of the moment thing."

He took her hand in his own, recalling the dream. "She's dangerous, luv. Fiona murdurred me, bit ah cam 'ere instead o' dying."

Catriona sighed. "She is the *worst*."

He chuckled and noticed for the first time that Catriona wore a long shirt and no pants.

"Ye've git nae pants on."

She glanced at her bare legs. "No kidding. I woke up with you screaming in here."

"Whit time is it?"

"Almost five. You slept for, like, twelve hours."

He rubbed his eyes. "Och. Ah guess ah did need mah kip." He grinned and pulled back the sheets. "Ye want tae hop in?"

Catriona laughed and stood, slipping her hand from his grasp. "Oh no, you don't. Get up and get dressed. We have a lot to do today." Her gaze roamed his chest. "You're all sweaty."

"Ah wis havin' a nightmare aboot the time ah wis stabbed tae death. Ye'd be sweaty tae."

She leaned forward to lightly touch the edges of the bandage beneath his left arm. "We'll have to change this and bag it again for your shower. I wish we had—" She paused, looking as if she'd remembered something.

"Whit?"

"I know where there's a tub—in the empty apartment across the hall. How did I forget that? Hold on."

Catriona strode from the room. Broch heard her leave his apartment and enter her own. He stood and wrapped his great kilt around his shoulders like a robe. By the time he'd relieved himself, Catriona had reappeared in his bedroom with a key in one hand and a squishy, golden ball with holes in it in the other.

"I got this sponge in a gift basket once but never used it," she said, shaking the squishy thing. "Follow me."

He followed. Catriona crossed the hall and used her key to open the door there. Inside was an apartment similar to his own; just as sparsely furnished, but larger. She walked into the bedroom and then into a bathroom as he shuffled along behind her. At the back of the room sat a large, footed tub. Catriona walked to it and turned on the water, testing it for temperature.

"Ooh, bubble bath. Bonus," she said, snatching a bottle from a nook inside the wall behind the tub. She poured a liquid directly beneath the running faucet. Broch took a few steps forward and peered into the tub to find it frothing with foam.

Catriona grinned at him. "You can use this tub to bathe until you're healed. You can sit in here and keep your wound above water."

"Bit ah lik' mah showers."

"I know you do, but they're a mess for that gunshot wound. Give this a shot. No pun intended."

Catriona stood from her perch on the edge of the bath and he could see something had changed in her expression. The faintest hint of a smirk had developed on her lips. She slid her hands under his draped kilt and across his chest to his shoulders, slipping the cloth from its perch on one side to expose his wound. Gently, she peeled away the bandage and tossed it in the trash.

Gliding her hand along his chest to his opposite shoulder, she pushed against the cloth, asking him to remove the makeshift shawl. He pulled his shoulder forward to resist.

She leered. "Come on. Drop it. Since when are you shy?"

The kilt fell from his shoulder and he grabbed it at his waist.

"Ah ken undress *myself*," he said, trying to appear cross. He spurred on his pretend irritation to keep from scooping Catriona into his arms and carrying her into the adjoining bedroom. He wasn't sure if he'd ever seen anything as wonderful as Catriona in an oversized t-shirt.

"Get in. I won't look." She turned her back to him.

He dropped his kilt to the ground and stepped into the tub, easing himself into the warm water.

Heaven.

The bubbles closed around him.

"Are you in?" she asked.

"Aye."

Catriona turned and smiled. "Look at you. You look like a commercial. All you need is a rubber ducky."

She turned off the water and dropped to her knees to

plunge the sponge into the bath. Her hands brushed dangerously close to his hip.

"Ah can take mah own bath," he said.

"I know." She reached across him to grab a bottle from the shelf. As she did, he could see the side of her breast through the armhole of her shirt.

"Keep the heid," he muttered under his breath. In his mind, he began to walk through the steps of fashioning a pothook to distract himself from his desire, but his eyes could still see. He watched Catriona, mesmerized by her movements as she poured soap into the sponge, squeezing it until it began to lather.

"Ah ken whit yer doin'," he said, his voice barely above a whisper. He looked upon the sheet of bubbles with gratitude. Were it not for them, he feared the surface of the water might look something like the picture of the loch ness monster Catriona had once shown him.

"I don't know what you're talking about," said Catriona. The skin on her neck and chest had grown flush. Her lips seemed fuller than usual. As if they were begging for him to kiss them...

He turned his head away from her.

Na. Dinnae give in. She's goan tae marry ye first if it's the last thing—

He felt something soft touch his chest and turned back to find Catriona cleaning the area around his wound, careful to avoid the stitches. The soft touch of the sponge on his tender flesh ran a thrill through his body. She moved on, dipping the sponge into the water by sliding it down his abs and then drawing the water up the undamaged side of his chest, stroking his shoulder.

Broch tilted back his head to rest it against the ledge of the tub, his eyes closed. He couldn't remember ever feeling as comfortable and aroused at the same time before.

"I need you to lean forward a bit so I can do your back," whispered her voice in his ear. He opened his eyes and found her face close to his, those full lips brushing his cheek.

He was losing the battle. He could feel it.

Dinnae leuk at her.

He closed his eyes again and leaned forward.

Think aboot somethin' else. Think aboot...Scootlund. He pictured himself galloping on his steed across the wild moors, his hips moving with the motion of the horse beneath him...

Och na. Dinnae think aboot riding. Fur the love of—

The sponge eased down his back and he groaned with pleasure.

He'd almost reined in his thoughts when Catriona kissed the back of his neck.

That's it.

His eyes sprung open and he grabbed her, pulling her into the bath. She screamed and fell on him, belly-to-belly and he kissed her to stop the racket. She kissed him back, clinging to him as he pulled her hips against him.

She slid across him, losing her purchase on his bubble-covered chest. She slipped. A second before impact, their wild eyes met. Both knew there was no stopping her momentum.

This is goan tae hurt.

Her elbow jammed into his bullet wound. Broch barked in pain. She scrambled to move, slipping face-first into the divot between his pecs.

His arms pinned, Broch feared she might drown there.

Her weight balanced on her nose, Catriona's arms rose from the bubbles like a bird about to launch. Sputtering, she grabbed the sides of the tub and hoisted herself up and back on her knees, straddling his shins.

Broch squeezed his eyes shut as the sharp pain beneath his arm subsided. When he opened them again, she was staring at him, panting, her wet white tee clinging to her breasts, her face dripping with bubbles.

"Things like this are always much sexier in movies," she mumbled, flashing a lopsided smile. "Are you okay?"

"Ah'm fine. Bit ah need tae gae noo afore we end up in an identical predicament."

He slid his legs up and stood, his hand covering his nether regions, and stepped out of the tub to grab his kilt. He wrapped himself with it.

"But you're not done with your bath," she said, the playful smirk he'd seen earlier returning for an encore.

He shook his head. "Ye're a temptress and ah willnae fall fer yer tricks."

"I think you just did."

"Och." He waved her away. "Ah'll meet ye in a bit."

He strode out of the bathroom and headed for his apartment. He wouldn't feel safe until his door was locked behind him.

When it was, he closed his eyes, leaned against the door, and took a deep, cleansing breath, picturing Catriona in her wet tee.

Mebbe marriage isnae sae important.

CHAPTER TWENTY-TWO

Catriona scurried back to her apartment leaving a trail of bubbly water in her wake.

So close. Almost had him.

It hadn't been right of her to trick him into the bath but all's fair...

Catriona removed her tee and dropped it into her bathroom sink with a slap, still grinning about the tryst that almost was. The way he'd lifted her like she didn't weigh a thing and dropped her into the bath. She didn't know what was more of a turn-on—him or feeling like she weighed nothing at all.

She twisted the knob of her shower and heard her phone spring to life in the other room.

Figures.

She jogged back into her bedroom and dove across her bed to reach the cell.

"Hello?"

"Do you have running shoes?" asked Sean on the other side of the line.

Catriona scowled. "Yes. Probably as new as the day I bought them. Why?"

"I need you to run a five-k today."

Catriona chuckled and pulled herself up to a sitting position, flashing her window a sidelong glance as she covered her naked body with a sheet. She had to remember at any moment *big sis* might be staring through her blinds with binoculars.

"That's funny," she said.

"I'm serious."

She scoffed. "Seriously on *crack*."

"Teena Milagros received another death threat that seems specific to a charity run she's in this morning. I tried to talk her out of participating but she wouldn't listen."

"So you want me to *run* with her?"

"You and Broch."

"Broch? Oh, that should be fun, trying to find him clothes for *this*. Do they make running gear in sasquatch? When is this nightmare?"

"Nine o'clock."

"*This morning*? Please tell me you're kidding."

"I'm not."

"But that's—" she looked at her phone. "That's like three hours away."

"Right, so you have plenty of time to find some clothes and get downtown."

"But I need, like, a month to *train*."

"I'll text you the details. I already have you registered."

Catriona fell sideways and planted her face in the pillow next to her, chanting.

No no no no.

She heard Sean's tinny voice calling her from her phone. "Cat? Catriona?"

"*Fine*." She put the phone to her ear again. "Fine. Consider it done."

"Be on your toes."

"See? This is hopeless. I didn't even know you were supposed to run on your toes."

"I mean bring a gun."

"Naturally. What's a fun run without a gun strapped to your tiny running shorts?"

"Be careful."

"Of course. Good-bye. You suck."

She hung up and closed her eyes. She'd nearly fallen back to sleep when her phone dinged. Sean had texted the directions as promised.

"It wasn't a nightmare," she grumbled.

No. It *was* a nightmare.

She took a quick shower and rummaged through her drawers and closet for things that could be considered 'running clothes' if someone drank heavily and squinted one eye. For practice, she jogged into her living room wondering if she had time for a cup of coffee.

Something *large* moved on her sofa and she yelped.

Broch sat up.

"Och wummin ye scared me tae death."

"Scared *you*? What are you doing lying on my sofa like some giant scruffy dog?"

"Ah tellt ye ah'd meet ye. Ye were in the shower so ah waited."

He stood and she saw he wore his kilt beneath a plain gray t-shirt. She hadn't yet deciphered what made a day a *kilt day* yet.

He clapped his hands together. "Whit ur we daen today?'

Catriona peeked into the jar that held her coffee and found it empty. Muttering under her breath, she turned to address the Highlander. "Well, assuming I don't drop dead of a heart attack in the first ten minutes, we have new plans. Sean wants us to run a race with Teena Milagros."

"Run a race? Whit happens if we win?"

"We get to feel good about ourselves, I guess. We're there to protect Teena. It's a fun run for charity."

"A fun run?"

"Oxymoron, right? That's what I thought." Catriona spooned a dollop of peanut butter from a jar and pressed it against her tongue. "Want some?"

"Aye."

She dug another spoon into the peanut butter and handed it to him.

"Breakfast of champions. I need to find you some clothes."

Broch said something that sounded like *hmmwrrrnnnlllowes* and it took her a moment to translate from peanut butter to English.

"You're wearing clothes, got it. But you can't run a race in a kilt."

"Ah hae in the past."

"I'm sure, but nowadays, you have to have the proper clothes and shoes, or the *runny* people lose their minds." She put the peanut butter jar back in the refrigerator. "Or they feel superior to you and I don't want to give them the satisfaction."

Broch handed her the licked-clean spoon. "How come Teena needs oor hulp?"

"Someone's threatening her. Who knows? Crazy fan, probably. We have to keep an eye out for trouble until the wacko moves on to his next obsession."

Broch nodded.

"We've got just enough time to get you some clothes." She grabbed her purse and her gaze fell to her untrendy shoes. "Maybe me, too."

Catriona drove them to the nearest open athletic store and found Broch size fourteen running shoes, sweat-wicking shorts, and a matching tank.

"You know what they say about big feet," she said as she

walked their booty to the checkout counter.

"Whit?"

She snatched two pairs of running socks from the display near the register. "Big socks."

One of the best things about Broch's time-traveling issues was she could use moldy-old jokes and they were always new to him.

She used the studio's credit card and asked if they could change in the store before leaving. Granted permission, they did so and then circled the fun run check-in area, searching for a parking spot.

Broch groaned as they made their third loop around the block. "It wid hae bin quicker tae donder fae the store."

Catriona growled as someone a block ahead of her found a spot. "I'm not walking a *foot* farther than I have to today."

After finding a spot, they hurriedly strode to the check-in table.

"Whaur am ah running tae?" asked Broch as Catrina pinned his number to his back.

"Back here. It's a loop."

He scowled. "Whit's the point o' that?"

"That's what I'm saying. That, and why would you run when you *own a car*?" She looked him up and down, admiring his body in the skimpy running outfit. "You look like you were born to wear that."

He winked. "Ye dinnae keek tae ill yerself."

Catriona spotted a short, curvy Latino woman and grabbed Broch's hand to drag him through the mingling racers toward her.

"Teena?"

The woman's head turned and her eyes flashed with fear.

"It's okay, I'm Catriona. Sean sent us." She hooked a thumb toward Broch.

Petite Teena tilted back her head to find Broch's face.

"You're enormous." She tapped her long, neon-orange nails on Broch's chest.

He nodded. "Sae ah've been tellt."

Teena hooted with laughter and grinned at Catriona. "I should feel safe around him, no?"

Catriona nodded. "We've got you covered."

"Okay, well, let's go, right? I want to be up at the front with the winners."

Catriona groaned.

Fantastic.

Teena wove her way through the crowd. Though her large hoop earrings seemed impractical to Catriona for jogging, she could tell the rest of the performer's skin-tight running outfit was top of the line. Catriona slid her hand across her crumpled running shorts, attempting to iron them with palm heat. At least she'd invested in a new racer-back tee. That made her feel official.

She glanced behind her to be sure Broch kept up as they made their way through the crowd. He nodded, acknowledging her attention. While he had all the right clothing now, his body type didn't say *runner*. He looked as though he'd made a wrong turn on his way to a rugby match.

Someone on a bullhorn suggested the runners gather at the starting line. Teena stretched, rising to wave at the crowd between deep waist-bends.

Catriona and Broch flanked her.

"Please tell me you aren't very fast," said Catriona.

Teena grinned and lightly pinched Catriona's cheek. "Depends how you mean, Chiquita."

After a few more announcements the starter's pistol blasted and the runners jumped forward like a panicked school of fish.

Four strides into the race, Catriona knew how much she was going to hate her day. Running had never been her *thing*.

While she'd never been rail-thin, she'd never felt the need to diet and exercise either. Her natural padding huddled in the right places. Her stomach was taught, her thighs didn't jiggle. She was young and nature hadn't turned on her yet. She'd done some cross-training for strength and endurance but running for the sake of running felt like *insanity*.

The crowd thinned as the faster runners stripped into the distance and slower runners fell behind. Teena had set a pace that put them somewhere in the middle.

Of hell.

Catriona looked over at Broch. He pounded along in his easy stride, his massive pecs bouncing with each step, mouth closed, still breathing through his nose like a pro. She felt like a goldfish, gasping for shrimp flakes.

Pay attention.

Catriona wiped the sweat from her brow and tried harder to study the people who lined the course, cheering on families and friends. She wasn't sure what to look for—it wasn't as if Teena's stalker would be carrying a flag that said *Here to hurt Teena.*

Maybe the attack would come in the form of another runner.

She looked around them. No one seemed suspicious. They'd picked a portion of the pack where everyone seemed hard-pressed to do anything beyond not falling further behind. Who among them had the extra strength to bother Teena? Not the bald guy on her left. He sounded as if he was about to give birth to a Great Dane.

As they approached a table filled with small paper cups, Teena swerved in front of Broch to grab a cup of orange liquid and down it.

Catriona scowled, sending the rivulets of sweat on her forehead squirreling in new directions.

Damn. Should I let her do that? What if the drinks are

poisoned?

Catriona reasoned there was no way for someone to guess which table Teena would use, let alone which cup she'd grab. A *nutcase* could poison *all* the cups, but that sort of dedication didn't happen often.

By the time Catriona had worked through all the probabilities of poisoning tiny cups of unnaturally colored sports liquid, they'd jogged far from the table and she realized she hadn't grabbed herself something to drink. Suddenly, her tongue felt twice the size of her mouth.

I should maybe jog more regularly.

They fell back into a rhythm. Catriona checked her smartwatch to find they were about halfway to the finish line.

"How are you doing?" she asked Broch.

He looked over at her, appearing as relaxed as if he'd been swinging in a hammock.

"Guid." His brow knit. "Ye keek a wee red in the face."

Catriona grimaced and picked up her pace. "I'm *fine*."

Teena glanced at her, grinning. "This is fun. Are you having fun?"

Catriona smiled. "Definitely. Think I'll go to the dentist after and make it my perfect day."

Teena gave her the thumbs up and returned to waving at the crowd.

Amidst the families and screaming supporters, Catriona spotted a figure in a baggy tracksuit with a large mop of blond hair obscuring his or her face. From the outfit, she guessed the person as male. Something about him felt *off*. He didn't cheer. His hands remained in his pockets, and only his head moved as he scanned the runners.

As they grew closer, the figure reached into a pocket and retrieved a neon-blue object. He pushed past one of the wooden barriers lining the course to enter the path of the runners.

Catriona looked at Broch and saw his laser gaze had already locked on the man. They exchanged glances and Catriona touched Teena's arm to slow her pace.

It's on.

As they approached, the man held up the object in his hand. The bright blue color didn't make sense to Catriona, but the shape of the weapon was undeniable.

"Gun!" Catriona shouted, pulling on Teena.

As they collapsed, a stream of liquid burst from the gun. Catriona had stopped their progress early enough to avoid the bulk of the spray, but a drop struck her leg as they fell. Pain erupted at the spot of contact.

Acid.

Teena screamed and clawed at her arm and Catriona spotted a sizzling spot of acid on the dancer's flesh. The crowd scattered, screaming. Runners stopped, only to be slammed into by others, a tangle of bodies piling behind them.

The gunman raised his weapon into the air and snaked back through the barriers with Broch close behind him.

Catriona spotted a man holding a bottle of water behind the barrier and she sprang from the ground to snatch it from his grip. Squirting it on the burning patch of skin on her shin, she dumped the rest on Teena's arm as she lay writhing, screeching in pain and confusion.

"It's acid, use water!" she screamed at a woman trying to calm a screaming friend. People ran forward with additional bottles and Catriona poured more on Teena's arm and her own leg.

Several people shouted they'd called 911. More people took photos for their Instagram accounts.

"It's okay. You're going to be okay," Catriona reassured Teena, doing her best to shield the actress from the crowd.

Teena   sobbed.

CHAPTER TWENTY-THREE

Broch whipped through the barriers after Teena's attacker, the blond ahead of him shoving his way through the crowd, sending people spinning. He couldn't call out to the crowd to help him stop his prey for fear the rogue still had his weapon. Stopping to steady the people shoved from the bastard's path also didn't help him close the gap.

Teena's attacker proved smaller and more agile than Broch had first suspected. The weasel broke through the crowd and sprinted unhindered down the street as the Highlander bumped his way through the startled onlookers. Reaching the edge of the mob, Broch bolted, taking a second to appreciate the feel of the cushioned shoes Catriona had purchased for him. It was as if he'd wrapped the more spongy areas of the moors around his feet.

The gunman turned left and scampered between two buildings. Broch reached the alley entrance and leaped over a blond wig lying on the ground. He caught a glimpse of his quarry turning the far corner.

Broch dashed to the end of the alley. A car door slammed shut nearby as his speed sent him spilling over the curb and into the street. A blue truck barreled toward him, launching from its parking spot at the curb. With no time to return to the safety of the sidewalk, Broch dodged forward into traffic.

The truck peeled past him as he spun to avoid being clipped by the large side-view mirror. A much shinier black truck screeched to a halt to keep from striking both him and the attacker's vehicle and Broch slapped his hands on its hood to steady himself.

The man inside the truck yelled at him and Broch held up a hand of apology as he made his way back to the curb. The old blue truck reached the end of the block, turned, and disappeared from view.

The man in the black truck continued to curse at Broch. Frustrated with his failure to capture the gunman, Broch spun and roared.

"Shut yer geggy afore ah pull ye oot o' thare 'n' snap yer neck, ye eejit!"

Startled, the man offered a final mutter and drove on.

Broch leaned against a building. Hands on his hips, catching his breath, he spotted the blue gun on the ground near where the truck had been parked. He removed his shirt and used it to retrieve the weapon, doing his best to preserve any fingerprints the way Catriona had taught him.

He walked the gun back to the scene, stopping to gather the wig as he retraced his steps.

Catriona spotted him as he approached the spot where Teena had been attacked. An ambulance had arrived and police began to tape off the area. Broch hovered outside the tape as Catriona jogged up to him.

"He got away?"

Broch nodded. "*Drove* away in a truck. Nearly bolted me doon." He held out his shirt and unwrapped the prize within. "Ah fund this, though."

"The gun? Nice. Be careful. It has acid in it. It'll burn right through your shirt." She pointed to his other hand. "What's that? A wig?"

"Aye. His real locks wis mirk 'n' short."

"Mirk? Oh, *dark*. I know that one now."

He grinned. "Yer a fine student."

She grinned and nodded to his finds. "Let's get that stuff to the police. There's an officer over there interviewing Teena."

Broch's eye fell to a bandage wrapped around Catriona's calf. "Yur hurt."

"It was a drop. I'm fine. The EMTs already fixed it up."

Broch ducked under the tape and handed the gun and wig to the police. It made him sad to lose his new shirt. He'd liked the slick feel of the fabric.

"Ah hud tae give mah new shirt tae the policeman," Broch whispered to Catriona.

Catriona chuckled. "We can get another."

"Guid."

Catriona made her way to the ambulance and Broch followed, bouncing in his shoes. He'd liked the jog but he'd *really* enjoyed the sprint pursuing the gunman. He felt as if he were standing on springs.

The EMTs prepared to load Teena into the ambulance. As Catriona approached, the woman's already red-rimmed eyes began to tear anew as she motioned to her bandaged shin.

"Catriona, look what he did to my legs. My *beautiful* legs."

Catriona took Teena's hand. "You'll be good as new in no time."

Teena sniffed. "It will scar."

"Teena, before you go, I have a quick question for you."

"*Anything*. You saved me." She looked at Broch and held out her other hand. "And you."

Broch took her other hand, unsure what to do with it. He followed Catriona's lead and patted the woman's fingers.

Catriona grew close to Teena. "Do you know a woman

named Jessie Walker? She's a makeup artist."

Teena scowled. "Yes, I know her. I had her fired from the show. She kept trying to lighten my skin with her powders. I told her I am a *Latina* woman, not the snowman Frosty. Then, when she poked me in the eye—I'd had enough."

Catriona nodded. "Okay. Thank you. You get better."

Teena's eyes flashed with rage. "Did *she* have something to do with this?"

The EMTs lifted Teena into the ambulance as she continued to call after Catriona.

"Did she? Did that little puta—"

The ambulance doors closed.

Catriona sighed and looked at Broch. "It's starting to look like everything revolves around Jessie Walker."

He nodded. "Aye."

CHAPTER TWENTY-FOUR

"He in?"

Kiki stared up at Sean from her desk outside Aaron Rothstein's office, mouth pursing and smiling at the same time as if she knew a secret and wanted Sean to pull it from her lips.

"Who wants to know?" she asked.

Sean grinned. "The man of your dreams."

"Where? Is he standing behind you?"

Sean chuckled and sat on the edge of the desk.

"If you let me in, I'll take you to dinner."

"I will not be bribed, Mr. Shaft."

"Well, it's pretty important, so I'm going in anyway. You might as well take the dinner."

Kiki offered him a theatrical sigh. "Fine, but I have to warn you. The chippie of the week is in there with him."

Sean's lip curled. "They're not...?"

"Who knows? He didn't ask me for his heart pills though, so you're probably safe."

Sean stood. "The Ivy?"

"Let's do Madeo. I could kill for pasta."

"Deal. Six."

"*Seven.*"

He pouted. "You're going to keep me up past my bedtime."

She blinked at him from beneath her strawberry bangs. "Would that be so bad?"

Trying to keep some semblance of cool, Sean slid from the desk and sauntered to Aaron's door, feeling in no hurry to leave Kiki behind. He knocked and, from inside, Aaron barked for him to enter.

"Sean!" Aaron held his arms out in welcome as Sean entered. "How's my favorite fixer?"

"I have news—"

Sean cut short as his gaze settled on the woman standing beside Aaron.

Aaron read his expression and put his arm around his trophy. "Sean, do you know Fiona Duffy?"

Fiona stepped forward, her hand held out to shake his. "I think our paths have crossed."

Jaw clenched, Sean shook her hand and turned his attention to Aaron. "I need to talk to you."

"You can say whatever you need to in front of Fiona."

"No. I *can't.*"

Fiona grabbed her purse. "It's okay, Aaron. I don't want to listen to whatever dreary studio business you need to talk about anyway. See you later?"

Aaron grinned like a schoolboy. "Of course."

He kissed her cheek and with a last smirk at Sean, Fiona left the office.

Aaron watched her leave as if he'd bought tickets for the event.

"She's something else, isn't she?" he asked.

Sean sniffed. "That's one way to put it."

"Keep your eye on her for me."

"Why?"

"She's our newest acquisition."

"She's coming to Parasol?"

"Not coming, *came*." He chuckled at a joke to which only he was privy. Sean didn't ask.

Aaron slapped Sean on the shoulder and walked around his desk to flop into his desk chair. "How can I help you?"

Sean found it hard to pull his gaze from the door through which Fiona had sauntered.

"Aaron, are you sure you want Fiona here?"

The man scowled. "Of course I'm sure. The girl's been on *fire* since the kidnapping thing. Bad girls are hot right now. Her prison time was gold."

"But—"

"It's *done*."

The tone of Aaron's voice dropped lower and Sean looked up to find the studio head glaring at him. He'd seen the look before.

Discussion time had ended.

Aaron leaned back in his chair. "Tell me the news."

Sean sighed and took a seat. "We've tied what happened to Colin, Timmy, and now Teena together."

"I heard about Teena. She's okay?"

"She's fine. Little acid burn on her leg. Quick thinking on Catriona's part neutralized the acid and Broch took care of the attacker."

"Caught the guy?"

"No. Scored some evidence but the guy got away. But, the attack ended quickly and no one else was harmed in any real way."

Aaron wove together his fingers and tapped his thumbs against each other, hands resting on his belly. "But you think there's a connection with Colin and Timmy?"

"I do. All of them worked with a makeup artist by the name of Jessie Walker. Pages from what reads like a diary of grievances showed up at both Colin and Timmy's houses, and I just got word back from my police contacts there's a pink page in bag inside the gun used to spray the acid.

"What's her problem, this Jessie Walker?"

"I don't know. She's gone missing. I tracked down a phone and address for her father, but I haven't been able to reach him. He might be involved."

"Why do you say that?"

"There was a shrine dedicated to Jessie at her apartment. A note about *avenging* her. People don't usually build shrines to themselves."

"So you think the father built it?"

"Could be. I'm going to send Catriona and Broch to his house in Rising Sun."

Aaron leaned forward. "Where the hell is that?"

"Out in the desert."

Aaron snorted. "Only a crazy person would live out there."

Sean frowned and stood to leave. "We'll know more when Catriona gets back. You should know Jessie Walker also worked with Fiona."

Aaron straightened. "You think she's in danger?"

"Could be. Colin broke up with her, Timmy disappointed her, Teena had her removed from her show—which led to her being fired from Parasol—and Fiona fired her from her freelance job at Hell Hound Studios. Could make her next in line."

Aaron ruminated on this new information before flicking his fingers in the direction of his door. "Find Fiona. Watch her until we get this Jessie girl or her dad or whoever's responsible."

Sean frowned, realizing the impact this new direction would have on his dinner date. "Any idea where she went?"

"I set her up with Doug's old trailer. I know she was

anxious to start redecorating. She's probably there."

He pressed the intercom button on his desk phone. "Kiki? Get Sean Fiona Duffy's home address."

"Will do," crackled Kiki's reply.

Aaron looked up. "Go. Keep her safe."

Sean nodded and left the office, attempting to look on the sunny side of his new assignment. Maybe spending more time with Fiona would allow him to better explore her connection to Catriona and Broch.

Kiki spotted the sour expression on his face the moment he entered the reception area.

"We're not having dinner, are we?"

"I'm going to have to raincheck it until our immediate problems are solved."

Kiki sighed. "Always solving everyone else's problems. Maybe I should hire you to fix *me*."

He took her hand in his and kissed the back of it. "You're already perfect."

She giggled. "Get out of here, you big sexy bastard."

Sean called Catriona on his way across the lot, digging the address Luther had given him for Jessie's father from his pocket as he waited for her to answer.

Catriona picked up. "Hello?"

"Hey, how are you both?"

"We're fine. Teena's fine too."

"I heard. You did a good job. Tell Broch I said so, too."

"Do I have to? It might be too early in his employment to shower him with praise, don't you think?"

Sean chuckled. "Just tell him."

"Fine. It's going to go right to his head."

Sean unrumpled the paper in his hand. "Listen, Luther found Jessie's father's address. He's in Rising Sun. I need you two to see if you can find him. Find out if Jessie is there."

"Rising Sun?"

He rattled off the address and she huffed.

"Why don't you just ask me to check on the moon while I'm at it," muttered Catriona.

He grunted. "You've still got a better assignment than me."

"Why? What are you doing?"

"I've been tasked to watch over the potential next victim."

"Who's that?"

"Fiona Duffy."

Catriona's shriek forced Sean to pull the phone from his ear.

"*Fiona*?"

"Yep. She's Aaron's new girlfriend and the studio's latest acquisition."

The phone went silent.

"Catriona?"

Her voice returned. "This is a nightmare."

"I'll give her your congrat—"

Sean stopped as he approached Fiona's new trailer. The door hung open, a smear of blood running from one side to the other. He pulled his gun from beneath his jacket.

"Cat, I'm going to have to call you back. Go see what you can find. Take Broch and your gun. I'll call you in a little bit."

"Is something—"

Sean hung up and dialed Luther.

"Luther, shut down all the exits. I might have a situation."

"Consider it done."

Sean pushed the phone into his pocket. Creeping to the door of Fiona's trailer, he poked his head inside.

The trailer was trashed. A small suitcase lay upended on the ground, shoes and clothing scattered around it.

Sean checked the bathroom and found it empty. He holstered his gun and redialed Luther.

"Be on the lookout for Fiona Duffy, or someone carrying something Fiona Duffy-shaped."

"Fiona? She ain't ours."

"She is now. Aaron's taken an interest."

"Damn. And we already lost her?"

Sean sighed. "Find out if anyone's seen any vehicles leave and do a full sweep of the lot. Let's see if we can find her before I have to tell Aaron his girlfriend's gone."

As he hung up, he noticed a pink piece of paper pinned to the wall beside the large lighted mirror.

Something in the mirror caught his eye and he turned.

Tucked in the corner of the sofa sat a cowgirl doll, smiling.

CHAPTER TWENTY-FIVE

"I thought I'd have heard from Sean by now," said Catriona. She and Broch had driven over two hours into the desert beyond Los Angeles to look for Jessie Walker at her father's house, the terrain growing more and more desolate by the minute.

They passed a derelict amusement park, its once bright colors fading in the desert sun. The giant sign out front announced it as The Okie-Dokie Corral, but the bulbs that once illuminated the words had broken long ago. A litter of white glass shards lay on the ground beneath the entrance. Catriona imagined kids had thrown rocks at the bulbs until they were gone. As a local kid, it would be hard not to.

A giant clown shaking in the hot breeze waved to them as they passed, his million-gallon cowboy hat half missing.

"Not creepy at all," mumbled Catriona.

Another ten miles down the road, Catriona slowed and crept into the driveway of a modest rancher home.

"I think this is it."

She shifted her Jeep into park, sad to see the home hadn't survived the desert any better than the amusement park had. She could see it had been years since the wooden home had seen a coat of paint. The few window shutters remaining hung at unnatural angles.

"Yikes." Catriona had never heard of a haunted rancher, but if it existed, this was the place.

She caught Broch studying her expression. "He's nae a wealthy man," he said.

"No. It appears Jessie came from humble beginnings."

As they made their way to the door, Catriona found herself patting the gun tucked into her waistband. Sean had asked her to bring it and now she was glad he had. The remoteness of the location made her feel uneasy. It had a real *this is where you go to die* feel about it. All they'd missed on the way there was a creepy old guy at a gas station warning them not to enter the shack.

The floorboards of the short front porch groaned as they crossed them to the door. She knocked, feeling Broch's presence behind her, the great bulk of him jutting like a rock in an ocean of dust and tumbleweeds.

"You don't have to stand that close," she murmured, feeling his breath on her neck.

"Ah'm yer backup, sae ah hae tae be up yer back."

She tittered. "You are such a *goof*. Back up a *little*. I don't trust these boards and if we go through them and end up stranded, living with a family of armadillos, I'm blaming *you*."

"Whit are armadillos?"

"They're like giant rats wearing suits of armor."

Brochan scowled and peered over the edge of the porch as if hoping to catch sight of the creatures.

Catriona knocked again, the screen-less door rattling beneath her knuckles.

"Mr. Walker?" she called.

An old Chevy truck sat parked on the side of the house, up on blocks, tires missing. The ancient vehicle didn't look as if it had moved from its spot for many years. Tumbleweeds were piled in the back tire well like a bird's nest.

As she stared, a snake appeared from somewhere at the back of the house to slither beneath the truck.

Catriona grimaced. "Do you have snakes in Scotland? Didn't St. Patrick drive them all out?"

"That's Ireland."

"Oh. Right."

"We hae adders. Or at least we did."

Nodding, Catriona returned her attention to the door.

I need to get out of this Mad Max nightmare.

She tried the knob. It turned.

She opened the door a crack.

"Mr. Walker?"

No response.

She pushed the door open farther, pressing her shoulder against the wood. It stuck on what she guessed used to be a shag rug. Now the floor covering resembled a greasy slick of blue putty.

She entered with Broch behind her, her fingers dancing on the grip of her Glock. The smell of the house didn't seem right, but then, she hadn't expected it to smell like a summer's day.

They stepped directly into a small living room with an old television deep enough to hold the complete works of Shakespeare and a sofa as threadbare as a pauper's jacket. Dust swirled in the beams of light filtering through the torn shades.

Broch's nose wrinkled. "It smells o' death."

"I'm guessing his housekeeper's quit."

Catriona glanced through the side window and felt her heart race. She'd spotted the abandoned truck again through a dirty window, and for a second, thought someone had pulled up to the house.

Sean had asked her to find Jessie's dad, but at the moment, Jessie's dad felt like the *last* person she wanted to see.

Catriona walked across the carpeted floor, each step bringing her closer to burning her shoes when she returned home. She peered into the kitchen. Dishes piled high around the sink. Something on the counter near the refrigerator caught her eye.

"Is that thing moving?" she whispered, pulling her gun and using it to point at what looked like a red, pulsing pile of insects.

"Aye."

Broch answered, but he didn't go charging across the kitchen to investigate.

"Shouldn't you check it out?"

He put his hand on his chest. "Me?"

"You're the big tough guy."

"If that wis a man aboot tae attack ye, ah'd break him in hauf, bit that's lik somethin' oot o' a nightmare."

They stepped forward together across the yellowing linoleum to inspect the object.

"Ants," they said in unison.

The ants had swarmed a half-made sandwich covered in mold. A jar of mayonnaise sat beside the sandwich with the lid off, growing a bumper crop of exotic plant life. As she watched, a cockroach skittered across the stovetop. Catriona yipped and recoiled, stumbling back toward the outskirts of the room, Broch steadying her as she went.

"Walker's bin gaen a while."

Catriona jogged in place, wiping imaginary critters from her arms.

"Agreed. Ugh."

When she'd rid herself of the willies, they pushed deeper into the house by way of a dim hallway. Passing a bathroom, Catriona poked her head inside, unwilling to investigate further. The torn shower curtain hanging against the wall revealed the grubby tub as empty, for which she would be forever grateful. She'd rather eat the ant sandwich than pull back a closed shower curtain right then.

Broch passed her and continued into the master bedroom at the end of the hall.

"Cat," he called.

Catriona closed her eyes and took a moment to steel herself.

Here it goes. I know there's going to be a body in here somewhere.

She entered the bedroom to find Broch staring at a wall covered with newspaper clippings, photographs and letters. While the frilly yellowing curtains implied a woman might have lived in the home at some point in the distant past, the items on the bureau were all men's; a comb, a razor, and bits of metal that Catriona imagined meant something to someone.

She studied the clippings posted to the wall and found they were all about Jessie. Her diploma from beauty school had been stapled next to a photo of a smiling girl wearing a graduation robe.

She took a few pictures of the collection with her phone. "This feels different from the shrine at Jessie's house. More natural. Like a memory board of some kind."

"Ah think some o' these gaed thare," said Broch, pointing at a few empty spots in the collage where the color of the original wallpaper had been preserved by something now missing.

"He took part of his collection here to her house to set up *that* shrine."

Pulling back a dusty curtain, she spotted a small barn in the backyard. The sidewall of the structure appeared darker than the front.

"I think his barn caught fire," she said, making out the streak marks where it appeared flames had licked a path.

They walked back down the hall, pausing briefly to

inspect a room stuffed with boxes and furniture. Beneath the clutter stood a bed covered by a pink comforter, but if the room had once been Jessie's, it had been a long time since she'd slept there.

As Broch jerked open the back door the unmistakable smell of burnt wood reached their nostrils. A red car sat parked near the barn.

"The roommate said Jessie had a red car," said Catriona.

They made their way down three cracked cement stairs and walked across the yard to the fire-damaged barn.

The frame of the structure had tilted, knocking the front sliding door from its track.

"See if you can get it open."

Broch wrapped his fingers around the door's handle and heaved, wood shifting far enough to allow them access. Catriona lifted a foot to move forward, only to have Broch wrap his arms around her and swing her away. The barn groaned as the door lost its tenuous hold on the tracks and collapsed beside them, kicking up a cloud that enveloped them in dust.

Catriona choked, her arms pinned by Broch's, her feet hanging a few inches from the ground.

"Put me *down*," she croaked.

He did and she covered her mouth to cough again, waving her other hand in front of her to clear the air around them.

Sunlight flooded the inside of the barn. Both their gazes fell on a large pile of ash in the center of the dirt-floored structure.

"Looks lik' some kind o' funeral pyre," said Broch, his eyes still watering from the dust.

Catriona sniffed and cleared her vision. The charred remains of a human body lay in the center of the ashes, a gasoline can by its side. Several melted trophies stood sentinel beyond the gasoline can, their marble bases the only recognizable parts left.

"Are those flower petals?" asked Catriona, stooping to grab what looked like a bunch of wilted carnations, tied together with a red ribbon.

Broch squatted beside the skull and pushed a bit of ash aside with his finger. "Dae ye think he burned his daughter?"

Catriona lifted a trophy. The words *High School* were still visible on the base's brass inscription plate.

She grimaced. Even with the destruction of the pyre, there remained something inherently feminine about the area. The dead flowers, pushed by the desert breeze, tumbled across the dirt floor.

She grimaced. "Feels like this was his final shrine to her."

Behind a wooden workbench in the back of the barn, Catriona spotted a sheet of the familiar pink lined paper, pinned to a pegboard.

Careful to avoid the piles of ash and trophies, she walked to the back and leaned forward to read the note aloud.

"The Diary of Jessie Walker."

The handwriting on the title page was even more flowery than the loopy print of the sheet they'd found in Timmy's dressing room.

Beneath Jessie's name, in an almost child-like print and different color of ink, someone had scrawled a second line.

My   sweet   baby   girl.

CHAPTER TWENTY-SIX

Cassidy sat in Jessie's father's truck stroking the hair on the doll. Gazing at the window of her apartment, she wondered if it was safe to gather the other dolls. Jessie's roommate should be at work.

She'd need them all.

Once she'd started thinking about it, she'd thought of a *bunch* of other people who'd ruined Jessie's life, starting with her mother. She'd left Jessie's father when she was a baby. That woman lived in Colorado now with a whole other family. All Jessie ever got from her was a Christmas card once a year.

It wasn't fair.

Cassidy scanned the area. The street had few cars parked on it. She studied each, searching for people inside. Nothing had been on the news yet about the body in the barn.

She shook her head.

Stop it. Stop worrying.

Jessie is dead.

She set the doll on the passenger seat and exited the car. Entering her apartment building, she reached the elevator at the same time as an old woman. The woman glanced up from shuffling through her mail and blanched. Cassidy smiled, stepped into the elevator, and turned.

The woman remained hovering outside the door, staring at her.

"Are you coming in, ma'am?" Cassidy asked, holding the door.

The woman shook her head. "No. I, I forgot something in the mailroom."

Cassidy shrugged and made a lasso motion above her head before pointing at the woman. "You have a cowgirl-cool day!"

The woman continued to stare as the doors closed.

Cassidy rode the elevator to her floor and entered the apartment. She flipped to the key on her ring for unlocking the bedroom, only to find the door ajar. Resting her fingertips on the door, she pushed it open. Splinters of wood jutted from the frame and lay scattered on the floor like pickup sticks. Someone had forced the lock.

She swept her gaze over the room. Things seemed the same as she'd left them. It hadn't been the police. They would have left evidence of their visit.

She glared down the hall at the roommate's door.

Maybe Sandy decided to let herself inside.

Cassidy entered the room and sat cross-legged on the floor in front of the shrine she'd built for Jessie. Tucked behind another photo, she retrieved a shot of herself, sitting on Cowboy Walker's knee as they practiced the Cowboy Walker and Cassidy show. Her mother had taken that photo before she abandoned them.

A wave of sadness washed over her.

Jessie's father looked so happy then.

Hanging her head, she pounded the back of her skull with her fist, careful not to smear her makeup.

Don't cry.

She picked up one of the small cowgirl dolls she'd dressed

and held it to her chest.

She couldn't shake the image of walking into the house, calling for her father. The television blared. Though she hadn't been home in some time, it seemed like any other day at her father's house.

Jessie had gone to tell her father about Jessie's terrible month. She'd been dumped by Colin Layne and spotted him with a new girl already—Cari, with the coffee-colored skin and wide eyes.

Cari. Now that girl carried Jessie's diary in her head forevermore, so she could read the pain she'd caused.

Cari. Bloating under Colin's house.

Jessie's father found a bloated, dead coyote behind the house once. He told his daughter how a body with no bleeding wounds decomposed faster. Stunk faster. Cowboy Walker knew a lot of cool facts like that.

The police had already found Cari. She heard it on the news. Colin was in jail now.

Cassidy smiled until the rest of Jessie's homecoming memory played on the theatre screen in her mind.

That day, Jessie had turned off the screaming television and called for her father. Turning the corner into the kitchen she saw him, crumpled on the floor. He'd been dead for a while. There would be no saving him. Blood or vomit had trickled from his mouth and stuck to the floor, leaving a dark stain on the yellow linoleum.

She didn't know if he'd suffered. Maybe he'd fallen to the ground, dead before his head hit the ground.

Maybe not.

They'd traveled everywhere together, until Jessie's mother tired of his meager paychecks and ran off. Jessie's father started drinking more and Cassidy grew too big to continue the act. No one wanted to see a man pretend to be a ventriloquist with a young woman on his knee, he'd said. She begged him to continue but he wouldn't have it. She'd worked on her makeup, sewn a more flamboyant costume, but nothing changed his mind.

It felt as though they were drowning together. The three of them, father, Jessie and Cassidy. Jessie had to move to escape.

The talents she'd honed in perfecting Cassidy Cowgirl's makeup translated well to Hollywood.

Until Teena fired Jessie for no good reason.

Jessie had been hungover, thanks to Timmy and his drug parties. After Colin dumped her, she'd mentioned the affront to Timmy Grey and he'd suggested she come to one of his raves. Said it would pick up her spirits.

She scowled at the memory.

Party.

It wasn't a party.

It was an *orgy*.

Jessie had been so sad, so messed up. Timmy and his friend had taken advantage of her. Lured her to the bedroom and filled her with drugs until anything they suggested seemed like a good idea.

Everything had seemed to her like a way to strike back at Colin.

When she showed up at work the next day, her hand shook so badly she poked Teena in the eye with an eyeliner pen. Not *bad*. She didn't *blind* her. But the diva screamed, furious and fussing. Made a whole thing about it. Sent her away.

A few hours later the call came from the studio and Jessie was fired.

She still had her freelance gigs, working for less famous clients like Fiona Duffy. When she saw Fiona the next day, it was as if the woman could read her mind. She saw how upset she was. She commiserated until Jessie told her everything;

how horrible Colin, Timmy and Teena had been to her.

It had been a shock to be released from Fiona's production the next day. Fired twice in two days—

Cassidy cocked her head.

Why?

Why *had* Jessie been fired from Fiona's show?

She'd serviced several of the ladies on that set, but none of them had complained...

Someone had to be responsible.

She wanted to know.

Now.

Cassidy pulled her phone from the little pocket she'd sewn on the inside of her vest and called her contact number for Hell Hound Studios.

"Hell Hound, how can I help you?" said a familiar voice on the other line.

"Miss Shelly?"

"Yes?"

"Jessie Walker. Makeup?"

"Right. I remember you."

Cassidy smiled.

She thinks I'm Jessie. Good.

Cassidy continued, dropping the cowgirl twang from her accent. "You let me know *my services would no longer be needed.*"

"Right."

"I was so upset, I forgot to ask *why*. Was it something I did? Or did they hire a full-time person?"

Shelly sighed. "Look, I liked you Jessie. I'll give it to you straight. Fiona Duffy said she wasn't happy with you."

"Fiona?"

"She's the biggest star we've got and what she says goes. Once she said she wouldn't work with you anymore, it didn't make sense to have you come in for the others when we had to find someone new for her anyways."

Cassidy stared at the wall, the voice on the other side of the line a low drone in her ear.

"Jessie? Are you there?"

She hung up.

Fiona *knew* how upset she was. *She'd* been the one talking to her about how she'd been wronged. To hear her story and then get her fired a second time—

She hit Fiona's speed-dial number on her phone.

"Hello?"

"Fiona? This is, uh, Jessie."

"Jessie who?"

"Jessie Walker? Makeup?"

"Oh right. What's up?"

"I wanted to let you know I was fired."

Fiona gasped. "Fired? How can that be? That's so *wrong*. You're so *talented.*"

Cassidy's eyes squinted.

Liar.

She did her best to lighten her tone and sound like the walked-on trash Jessie was.

"Maybe you could tell them that and help me get my job back?" she asked.

Fiona hummed. "Oh, you know, I would, but I left Hell Hound. I'm with Parasol now. You should see my trailer. It's going to take me all day to redecorate. Super busy."

"But—"

"I have to go. Lots to do here. Good luck with everything. You deserve *so* much better. Bye."

The phone clicked dead.

Cassidy stared at the ground. She squeezed the head of the doll in her hand until the plastic cracked, and she felt the sharp bite of it slicing her palm. Dropping the doll, she raised the wound to her lips and pressed her tongue against the blood to stop it. Spit was a natural coagulant. Cowboy Walker told her that.

"Jessie?"

Cassidy turned at the sound of the voice. The roommate, Sandy stood at her doorway. The girl gasped, her hand rising to cover her mouth.

"Why do you look like that?"

"Look like what, partner?"

Sandy offered a nervous giggle. "You're crazy. Are you *acting* now?"

Cassidy stood and began gathering her other dolls.

Sandy continued. "Your sister was here looking for you."

Cassidy straightened. "Who?"

"Your sister and her husband. That guy is gorgeous. He had this accent—"

"I don't have a sister," said Cassidy.

Sandy scowled. "You don't? I'm sure she said she was your sister. I wouldn't have let her into your room otherwise."

"You let her into the room?"

"Yes, I mean, *no*, not really. They tried the door and it was open."

"It wasn't open, partner."

"They opened it. It took, like, two seconds. Though now that you mention it, it looks kind of messed up..."

"What did they want?"

Sandy shrugged. "They were looking for you. They were worried about you."

Cassidy took a deep breath. She wouldn't be able to come back if people were stopping by. They had to have seen the shrine, but they didn't call the police.

Why?

"Did they give you a name?"

"His name was Broch. He was British or something, but not posh-like, like, *manly*... Ooh, Scotland. That's right. I know you like those skinny, pretty boys like Colin, but this guy..."

Sandy's voice devolved into a drone in the back of Cassidy's head. She scanned the room, searching for anything else she might need going forward. She grabbed a spare makeup case and sewing kit and threw them into a suitcase with the dolls. She didn't need any other clothes. Cassidy Cowgirl always wore the same outfit. It was the best outfit for ropin' and ridin'.

"Are you moving out?" asked Sandy.

Cassidy pushed past her and headed for the door.

"Are you going to be back to pay next quarter's rent?" called Sandy behind her.

About to reach for the doorknob, Cassidy lowered her suitcase to the ground and turned.

Sandy had been following, but she stopped at the end of the hall, touching the wall to steady herself.

"Why are you looking at me like that? You're kinda creeping me out."

Cassidy put one foot forward, shifting her weight there.

Sandy was the only person who knew Jessie well.

Cassidy ran at the girl.

Sandy yelped, scrambling to run back down the hall to her room, but Cassidy was on her like a mountain lion.

Mountain lions and cougars are the same animals.

Sandy probably doesn't even know that.

She grabbed the girl's shirt and, spinning her, slammed her head against the wall. They fell together and Cassidy pinned Sandy, straddling her back, driving her head into the floorboards again and again.

She spat the words in time with the sound of Sandy's head striking the floor.

"I—told—you—stay—out—of—my—room—"

Panting, Cassidy rocked back on her knees. Blood had begun to pool beside Sandy's head.

Cassidy stood, watching Sandy for movement. Satisfied, she returned to her suitcase and retrieved one of the finished dolls. One that had a dark line dropping from each corner of its mouth to the chin, just like Cassidy herself.

She walked the doll to Sandy's unmoving body and dropped it on her back.

Cassidy   should   get   credit   for   this   one,   too.

CHAPTER TWENTY-SEVEN

From the barn where they'd found Jessie's burned remains, Catriona and Broch stared back at Walker's horrible house.

"Whaur dae ye think the bastard bolted?" asked Broch.

Catriona shook her head. "I don't know. I'm wondering why he would systematically hurt everyone who hurt Jessie, when clearly, he's the one who hurt her the most."

"Mibbie he didn't murdur her. Mibbie she died."

Catriona considered this. "That's possible. Maybe she came home after losing her job and killed herself. Maybe he blames the people he thinks drove her to it."

Catriona pulled her phone from her pocket to call 911 and groaned.

"No signal." She glanced at the house. "I think I saw a landline inside. Lucky Sean's such a dinosaur or I wouldn't have known what a landline looks like."

Catriona walked toward the house watching her phone as she moved. As she neared the back door, a single connection bar appeared.

"Nevermind. Got it."

She called 911 as Broch wandered around the yard and peered into the red car.

When she hung up, she found Broch staring at the ground beside the house.

"What's up?"

Broch twisted to look behind him. "Keek 'ere."

He pointed to the ground leading away from the back steps and toward the side of the house. A path had been smoothed in the dirt with two deeper lines running parallel inside the track.

"Drag marks?" asked Catriona.

"Aye. Someone dragged a body."

She pointed to the deeper grooves. "Heels?"

"Aye. Whoever did the draggin' wasn't strang enough tae pull the body wi' ass, legs 'n' heels draggin'."

They followed the path around the corner of the house. Next to the spot the drag marks ended, the lattice that surrounded the foundation of the house had been cut. The heel marks led beneath the house.

Bracing herself for the worst, she turned on her phone's flashlight and shined it beneath the house. The heel marks led a few feet inside, but she saw no body.

She wiped her brow. "Nothing."

Broch had left her side, scanning the ground as he walked back toward the barn.

"Where are you going now?"

"More tracks." He followed them to the barn and then turned to look back at her.

"Someone changed thair mind. Thay fetched a wheelbarrow 'n' teuk the body tae the barn."

"So he killed her—or found her—in the house, panicked, considered hiding her *under* the house, and then decided to give her a ceremonial burial?"

Broch shrugged. "Aye. Cuid be." He squinted into the distance.

Catriona put her hands on her hips. "What is it? You've

got that *staring across the moors* thing you do when you're thinking."

"Och. It's just the person bein' dragged wis *heavy*."

"How heavy?"

"Ah dinnae ken. Heavy enough the person draggin' hud tae lea the ass oan the ground."

"Jessie wasn't very large."

"Na. That's whit's got me thinkin'."

His gaze turned to the barn and she followed suit.

"You don't think it's her in the barn," she said, guessing what he was thinking.

"Na. Ah dinnae."

Catriona strode to the barn with Broch alongside her. She stood over the burned skeleton, biting her lip, unsure how to proceed. It did seem big to be Jessie's but it was hard to tell.

"Okay, we don't want to touch anything, but see if you see anything that says this was a man or a woman."

They hovered over the body, peering around the bones and ashes without disturbing the pile.

Catriona huffed. "What *is* the difference between a male and female skeleton?"

Broch grinned. "Female skeletons wear dresses."

"Very funny from the guy who practically lives in a skirt—Ooh, *here*." Catriona tapped away a piece of debris with her finger to reveal a shattered timepiece.

"It's a big watch. It could be a man's." Catriona clucked her tongue. "But not necessarily. Girls like to wear big watches nowadays."

They heard sirens approaching.

Catriona straightened. "Shoot. Step back a little. We don't want them to think we were messing with the evidence."

A police officer rounded the side of the building with his gun drawn.

"You in there," he called to them.

Catriona raised her hands and elbowed Broch to the side motioning to him to follow her lead.

"I'm the one who called," called Catriona.

The officer walked forward, his gun lowering. "Is there anyone in the house?"

"No. It's just us here. And this." She nodded her head toward the charred skeleton.

EMTs' appeared behind the officer, who holstered his gun and scanned the small barn.

"It's clear," he told them before turning to Catriona and Broch. "Follow me out here and let them do their thing. I need to ask you some questions."

Catriona nodded. "I have a quick question for the EMT if you don't mind." She locked eyes with the first tech to enter, a stout man in his forties with gray lining his temples.

"Can you tell if that's a woman or a man?" she asked.

He scowled. "Depends on what's left. There aren't many differences and this body is pretty much dust but...it isn't very large, which leans me toward female..."

Catriona frowned and glanced at Broch. "I guess it is Jessie."

She was about to head to the officer when the EMT spoke.

"Hold on. The pelvis is mostly intact and isn't very wide—"

Catriona spun on her heel to face him. "That's important?"

The man nodded. "Yeah. That's the main way to tell." He scratched his head. "These bones are in bad shape, but if I had to put money on it, I'd say this is a man. A short man."

Catriona removed her holster and tossed it in the Jeep, before leaning against the vehicle to watch the police mill in and around the Walker house of horrors. The cops were done with Broch and her, but she'd wanted to wait before leaving, on the off-chance her EMT friensd might have some additional information.

She kicked the dirt, sick of looking at it all. "I should have held off calling the cops a bit longer. If I'd known we were looking for Jessie instead of her father, I might have seen things in the house a little differently."

Broch's gaze swept the desert landscape. "Whit happened tae a' the *green* in this place?"

Catriona chuckled. "Kind of like looking at the corpse of Scotland, I imagine." She lifted her phone and flipped through the photos she'd taken in the Walker house, zooming in on each item pinned to the bedroom wall.

On the bedroom wall, there'd been an unusual number of photos of a ventriloquist dressed in a cowboy outfit, complete with an oversized twenty-gallon hat, boots, and chaps with fringe. Walker often sat with a large female dummy on his knee. The dummy's outfit paralleled his, its shirt fringed and skirt ruffled, long dark hair sometimes loose, sometimes in braids. A banner in the back of one of the photos identified the duo as Cowboy Walker and Cassidy.

The photo reminded her of the dolls they'd found at Jessie's house and the one on Timmy's bed. The doll meant something to the walkers.

Catriona couldn't shake the uneasy feeling creeping up her spine. She'd never been a fan of dolls, but ventriloquist dummies took things to a whole other level.

"Hey Kilty, check this out," she said, tapping his arm. "Does anything about this photo hit you as odd?"

He tossed a stone at a piece of scrub brush and glanced at the phone. "Tis a man with a girl on his lap."

"No, that's a dummy. A sort of doll."

He looked again. "Nae. Tis a wee lassie."

Catriona zoomed in on the dummy's face and gasped.

He was right. The way the eyes were looking—it wasn't a doll.

"Oh my God, you're *right*. It's a girl made up to *look* like a ventriloquist dummy. Holy—they had an act—Jessie and her father—a fake ventriloquism act."

Broch threw another stone. "Whit's the word ye blethered? Ventra-kissed?"

"Ventrilo*quist*. A ventriloquist is a person who talks without moving their mouth, while moving the mouth of a puppet, so it looks like the doll is talking."

"Sae the fowk peepin' think the doll is alive?"

"That's the effect, but no, they *know* the voice is the ventriloquist's."

"It's fae children?"

"Not all the time. Adults watch them, too."

Broch scowled. "How come wid a body watch a grown man pretend a doll is blethering?"

Catriona navigated to a clip of a well-known ventriloquist on her phone and let Broch watch the clip. As the man and the dummy bantered back and forth, Broch's expression broadened.

"Och. He tells jokes."

"Right."

Broch scoffed. "Ye kin bether jokes wi'oot a doll."

Catriona gave up, confident the charms of ventriloquism were lost on the Highlander. Her attention drifted back to the house.

She closed her eyes and pictured walking through Walker's home. Nothing in the living room. She moved on to the memory board and studied the photos and clippings. One newspaper image caught her eye; a girl swinging a lasso over her head.

Jessie Walker 'circles the wagons' as Cassidy was the caption.

How did I miss that? Jessie was older in that photo. The ventriloquism act must have been over for years by then, but perhaps she'd revisited it for special occasions. 'Circling the wagons' must have been a lasso trick of hers.

Catriona mentally walked into Walker's kitchen. There was the moldy mayonnaise and the half-made sandwich covered in—

Half-made.

That was it.

Something interrupted him.

Was it Jessie? Did she attack him? Hit him with something and knock him to the ground...

In her mind's eye, she glanced at the kitchen floor.

A chunky stain. The kitchen had been so filthy, and she had been so distracted by the ants, the stain on the floor hadn't stood out to her then. It wasn't spattered like blood. It was more concentrated...*larger.*

Walker might have laid on his floor for some time. He could have died while making a sandwich, fallen to the floor, rotted for weeks, months even, melting into the floor.

She tapped Broch again and he stopped his rock toss in mid-throw to look at her.

"I have a theory," she said.

"Aye?"

"I think Jessie's father was dead when she got here."

"Tis common here tae burn yer deid?"

Catriona grimaced. "No. Follow me a second. Maybe Jessie, already upset with her professional and romantic life, returned to the one man she trusted, only to find him dead. It gave her an idea. First, she thought she'd hide his body, and then changed her mind. Instead, she burned his body, doing her best to make it look as if her father had burned *her.* Then she returned to L.A. and created the shrine to herself to make it look as if her father had come to avenge her."

"But she's the one killin'."

"Exactly."

Broch nodded. "Na one wid be keekin' fur her if she were deid. They'd be keekin' fur her *faither.*"

"Right. She probably got the idea for the shrine from her father's real-life memory board in there. The problem for Jessie, even with her father burned nearly to dust, the medical techs were able to tell the body was male, no matter how many flowers and ribbons she left around it."

Broch sighed. "Somethin' in that wee lassie's mind broke."

"Considering she's been dressing herself up like the doll she used to be, I'd say it seems like it, doesn't it?" Catriona headed for the Jeep's driver-side door. "We need to get back to L.A. before she kills someone else."

CHAPTER TWENTY-EIGHT

Fiona opened her eyes, her head throbbing in time with her heartbeat. Her shoulders ached. Her face was pressed into a rough blanket, the surface beneath felt hard as cement. A heavy canvas covered the length of her body, leaving her unsure if it were day or night.

Her limbs felt *wrong*. Trying to sit up, she realized her hands were tied behind her back and her ankles tied to her hands, knees bent. She lay on her side. Her body jostled at uneven intervals, sometimes violently.

I'm in a vehicle.

She felt the wind through gaps in the canvas.

I must be in a truck bed.

Fiona swallowed and tried hard not to panic. Her inability to move her arms and legs had her on the edge of hysteria. She didn't like being pinned.

I'm hogtied in the back of a pickup truck.

She'd made jokes about ending up this way while filming *Camping Under the Stars.* Some of the locals in their rural filming location *looked* the sort to hogtie women and throw them in the back of their trucks.

Maybe one of them heard me and decided to make my joke

come true.

She swallowed and tried to push her mind elsewhere.

Calm. Breathe in and out. In and—

The truck slowed and turned left. Fiona's head bounced on metal and she did her best to lift it.

I can't take much more of this.

The truck rolled to a stop and Fiona realized there was something worse than being jostled in the back of the truck.

Knowing someone was on their way.

She heard a door open and close. Footsteps on gravel. The tailgate screeched open. Though she couldn't remember if she'd heard the back of a pickup truck open before, she imagined newer models didn't make a sound akin to banshees screeching.

She lay in a very *old* truck. For some reason, that raised her already elevated heartbeat another ten beats per minute.

The canvas slid from her body and Fiona saw it was dusk. She blinked and peered at the person standing at the back of the truck.

Her kidnapper had long dark hair beneath a cowboy hat. Thin shoulders, what looked like a skirt...

I was kidnapped by a woman?

The woman had her back turned to Fiona as she folded the canvas.

Fiona took a deep breath.

Okay. I can work with this.

Her abductor wasn't a three-hundred-pound, bearded monstrosity in dirt-encrusted overalls out to collect breeding specimens for his hill people. This girl was already a hundred notches up from Fiona's worst-case scenarios. She glanced up, straining her neck, attempting to see into the front cabin.

Unless this girl's boyfriend is still in the truck.

She couldn't see.

Surely this little girl hadn't carried her off the Parasol

Pictures lot by herself?

She couldn't recall the kidnapping. She remembered walking into her trailer, a blow to the back of her head, falling, thrashing—her vision darkened, the pain in her head unbearable—and then nothing.

Let's try working from a position of strength.

Fiona cleared her throat.

"Turn around, you coward."

The woman stopped folding the canvas and straightened.

"You cut me loose immediately. Do you have any idea who I am?"

The woman turned, and though Fiona thought she'd prepared herself for anything, she heard herself gasp.

Dark lines dropped from either side of the cowgirl's mouth, mimicking the hinges of a ventriloquist dummy's jaw. White half-circles beneath each eye created the illusion of a dummy's googly eyes. Dark shadowing beneath the cheekbones and above the eyes, in combination with hair-thin brown lines painted on her skin, made it appear as if she'd been carved from wood.

She wore a white shirt with frills at the throat, a brown vest with elaborate red stitching, and a long turquoise skirt. Cowboy boots peeking from the frills of her skirt completed the outfit.

Most worrisome, her clothing and face appeared smeared with dabs of blood.

Is that my blood?

"I know who you are, partner. You fired Jessie."

Still stunned by the vision of her captor, it took Fiona a moment to respond.

"What?"

"You fired Jessie. You knew she was in a rough place and you fired her."

Jessie. The makeup girl.

Fiona squinted.

It's Jessie under that makeup.

"Jessie?"

"No, my name's Cassidy. Cassidy Cowgirl. Jessie asked me to take care of you. Give you what you deserve."

When the girl spoke, only her chin rose and fell, the rest of her face remained frozen like a doll's. Her eyes rolled left and right, and up and down, but never at an angle. Jessie had clearly spent some time perfecting her Cassidy Cowgirl ventriloquist doll routine.

Fiona swallowed.

The girl's lost her mind.

She'd known Jessie Walker was on the edge. She'd given her a little push to see what would happen...but the chaos she created wasn't supposed to blowback on *her*.

"Who told you I fired Jessie?" she asked, playing along.

"Miss Shelley."

Fiona grit her teeth. *Shelley. Stupid trash bitch.* Talk about people she was going to fire...

She shook her head as best she could with her cheek against the bed. "Shelly had it wrong. You know I love you, er, *Jessie*. I *love* your work. I mean, look at your face now. You did that right? You're *amazing*."

Cassidy pulled what looked like a real six-shooter from a gun belt Fiona had somehow overlooked.

"Jessie don't—"

The girl raised her hand and shot into the sky.

"My name isn't Jessie! It's Cassidy Cowgirl! And you're a big fat *liar!*"

Jessie roared the last word, but it was the gun blast that made Fiona's head throb anew. Her ears rang. She realized Jessie's willingness to shoot into the open sky meant they were miles from anyone who might hear the explosion.

That didn't bode well.

Don't piss her off. If she wants to be Cassidy, go with it.

"Okay. Sorry. Cassidy. You don't want to hurt me. I'll get Jessie's job back. Okay? Let me go and I'll call the studio right now and get your job back for you. I mean, *her* job."

"I'm afraid it's too late for that, partner."

"Look, just let me—"

"You've said it loud as a dinner bell, Miss Fiona. You don't *want* to be pretty anymore."

Fiona felt her stomach flip with a sudden rush of nerves. "What? Wait—"

Jessie holstered her gun and collapsed at the waist like a marionette whose strings had been dropped. After a couple of seconds, she straightened and raised her hand over her head, her fingers gripping the handle of the largest knife Fiona had ever seen.

She must have pulled it from her boot.

This crazy bitch has weapons all over her body.

Cassidy Cowgirl's head tilted and, grinning, she winked with exaggerated force.

"Ready,   partner?"

CHAPTER TWENTY-NINE

Catriona pulled out of Walker's driveway. The police had left but for one cruiser, and the driver of that car had insisted they leave before he did. She'd wanted to loiter a bit longer, maybe take a run through the house again with Jessie Walker in mind instead of her father.

The cop didn't like that idea.

As Catriona pulled away from the house, grumbling, her phone rang and Broch answered it.

"Aye, this is Catriona's phone ye've reached."

Catriona rolled her eyes.

"Aye...Aye...Och... Aye. Whit? Och...Aye...Ah'll tell her. Aye."

He hung up.

"Who was it?"

"'Twas Sean. He says Fiona's been taken."

"You didn't tell him we think it's Jessie we're looking for and not her father?"

"He kens."

"How?"

"Jessie attacked Sandy."

"The roommate?"

"Aye. A neighbor found her and the lassie tellt the police Jessie harmed her."

Catriona nodded. Sean's never-ending network of police contacts had come through again. "That confirms what we suspected. How does he know Fiona was taken?"

"Her trailer wis mussed and there wis blood—"

"What do you mean her *trailer*?"

"She wirks fer Parasol noo."

"What?" Catriona worried her screeching voice might crack the windshield. "How is that possible?"

"She's..." he trailed off. Catriona glanced at him.

"Are you trying to remember a word?"

"Aye. *Datin'*."

"She's dating someone? Who?"

"Aaron?"

"*Aaron*?"

Catriona dropped her forehead to her steering wheel, happy the desert roads were straight and devoid of traffic because she feared she'd lost the strength to lift her head.

"It isn't bad enough she's looking over us like some twisted god—now she's *queen of the studio*?"

"Whit dae ye mean, keekin' o'er us?"

Catriona flicked her wrist in the air, pointing to a building she could only see in her memory. "She bought an apartment in that big white building behind the studio. She can see in our windows from there if she wants to."

Broch frowned. "Och."

"*Och* is right. I think she inspired some guy to try and murder his family to get it, too."

Broch scowled at her. "*Whit?*"

"I think I've pieced together what she does. What she *is*. You know how Sean said the three of us need to help people?"

"Aye."

"I think she's the opposite. *She* inspires pain and chaos.

She nurtures the wicked in people. Encourages them to do bad things."

"And nae she works fae *oor* studio?"

"Yeah. That can't be good. And our studio president is *sleeping* with her. She's ruining our lives just being *near* us—Aaron's in real trouble if he's f—" She cut short. "You get the idea."

In the distance, Catriona saw the crumbling Ferris wheel of Okie-Dokie Corral rising into the dimming light of day and tried to remember how long it had taken them to reach that point on the way to Walker's house. The math made her groan. They were still *hours* away from home.

She pressed the gas pedal. As much as Fiona's presence disrupted their lives, she didn't wish her sister dead. She needed to find her kidnapped ass, even if it was only to kick it.

As they passed the Okie-Dokie she noticed a faded blue pickup truck parked outside the gates. Her foot released from the gas and they began to slow.

"Whit's wrong?" asked Broch.

Catriona eased to the side of the road.

"Did you see the truck parked outside the old amusement park?"

He hooked a thumb toward the passenger window. "Na. Ah wis keekin' oot 'ere at this tairrible land."

Catriona ran through her memories of the photos they'd found at Walker's house until she located the image of Jessie leaning on the back of a truck, a tufted piece of grass hanging from her teeth. The truck was blue, a bit brighter than the one she'd seen parked at the gates, but very similar. She could see the license plate—A86K4R.

"Jessie's car was left at her father's but she wasn't there. She must have taken his truck when she left."

"The one ye saw back there?"

"I'm thinking it might be. I have to check."

She made a U-turn and rolled back to park beside the blue Chevrolet.

A86K4R.

"It *is* Walker's truck. She's *here*."

Catriona tucked her gun into the back of her waistband and jumped out of the Jeep. She jogged to peer into the back of Walker's truck while Broch inspected the cabin. A pile of canvas and a blanket were the only things in the open bed. She pulled on the canvas and spotted a hunk of cut rope and a splotch of what looked like blood.

"She could have stashed Fiona back here."

Broch shut the driver's side door. "There's nae sign of Fiona in 'ere."

Catriona pulled out her phone. "First we call the cops and then we tell Sean to check Parasol's tapes for a blue Chevy—*dammit!*"

No bars.

"Stupid desert."

She made as if to throw her phone, thought better of it, and instead shoved it back into her pocket for a timeout.

She turned and spotted a hole in the fence where someone had snipped the wires.

She motioned to the tear. "We're on our own. You think you can get through there?"

Broch strode to the fence and bent back the cut flap as if the thick wire was made of spaghetti.

Catriona felt that embarrassing flush of giddiness she suffered whenever manly men did manly things.

"That's a neat trick. You'll have to teach me," she said, hoping humor would distract him from her scarlet cheeks.

He rolled his eyes. "Aye. Ye gae first."

Catriona scrambled through and Broch followed, easing his bulky frame through with care to avoid catching his flesh on the exposed wire.

Brushing off her hands, Catriona scanned the crumbling park. A cartoon pig with peeling paint and a missing eye leered at her, pointing her toward the shuttered ticket booth.

"I've had nightmares like this place," she mumbled.

"Ye gae left and ah gae right?" suggested Broch.

Catriona shook her head. "There were pictures of Jessie and her father at a place like this. It makes sense she'd consider it a safe spot if they performed here. We need to find the stage she used to—"

A scream echoed through the park and the two of them froze.

Catriona felt the hair on her neck stand at attention. The scream hadn't been the shriek of a thrill-seeker on a plunging rollercoaster. It wasn't even the soundtrack of a woman afraid of her captor.

Someone   was   in   pain.

CHAPTER THIRTY

Catriona and Broch sprinted toward the sound of the scream. The deserted park proved shallow. Rounding a ride called *The Bucking Bronco*, which looked more like *The Creeping Spider*, they stopped, each flinging out an arm to halt the other.

Two women occupied the stage of a crumbling amphitheater. Though the red paint had faded to light pink, Catriona recognized the stage as the backdrop of some of the photos they'd seen in Walker's house. Cowboy Walker and Cassidy Cowgirl had entertained on that stage long ago.

An unwilling participant in today's performance, Fiona Duffy sat bound to a simple wooden chair. Another woman in a bright turquoise ruffle-bottomed skirt stood over her. The white shirt beneath a leather vest, the long hair, the cowboy hat—Catriona knew they'd found Jessie Walker.

A.K.A. Cassidy Cowgirl.

Metal flashed in the cowgirl's hand as she shifted, revealing the river of blood sheeting down Fiona's chin and neck. The blood-curdling scream they'd heard had been Fiona's. Jessie had cut her, somewhere near her mouth.

"Get away from me!" Fiona's body jerked as she kicked against the rope binding her feet to the chair, the words escaping in staccato bursts between racking sobs.

Undeterred, Jessie moved in, knife raising to Fiona's face as the actress's head thrashed, neck twisting to jerk her flesh away from Jessie's blade.

Catriona ran down the aisle of the amphitheater, raising her hands to her mouth to create a makeshift megaphone.

"Hey!"

Jessie's head snapped in her direction. She placed her large hunting knife against Fiona's throat and Catriona caught herself on a rusted audience chair to stop her momentum. Without turning her head, she shifted her eyes left and right, searching for her partner. Broch hadn't followed her down the aisle.

They didn't go down the aisle together.

The irony wasn't lost on her.

Maybe she'd share that joke with Broch if they managed to bring Fiona home with her face still attached to her skull.

Catriona resisted the urge to turn her head and look for the Highlander, unwilling to alert Jessie to the presence of another person in the park. If they had the advantage of surprise, they needed to keep it.

She held up her hands to demonstrate she had no weapon. Her gun felt too far away, tucked in the back of her jeans.

Catriona swallowed.

I can do this.

She'd talked enough of the studio's assets off ledges, both real and metaphorical, she felt she should be able to handle one troubled cowgirl.

"I'm not here to hurt you," she called out.

Jessie straightened, shifting her knife to her opposite hand to keep it poised at Fiona's throat. She tilted her head, mechanical in her precision.

Catriona's skin crawled.

Oh no. Don't start that stop-action horror film stuff.

Close enough now to see more detail, Catriona tried not to gape at Jessie's ventriloquist dummy makeup. The dark lines on either side of her mouth, the white semi-circles beneath her eyes simulating the wide eyes of a doll, the wood grain painted on her cheeks and forehead—any charm the little girl once possessed as a talking dummy had been stripped from this perverse replica. The blood smears on her face and clothing made the grotesque vision of Cassidy Cowgirl's past glory all the more horrifying.

"Who are *you*, partner?" asked Jessie.

The sing-song quality of Jessie's voice contrasted with the ghastliness of her visage left Catriona momentarily speechless.

"I, uh, I'm Catriona."

Catriona felt certain Jessie's dismissal from Parasol Pictures had contributed to her mental break and feared mentioning her affiliation with the studio might further disturb the girl. She had to find a way to keep her talking and distract her from Fiona.

"Wow, you look amazing," she said, walking forward, her hands still in the air. "Can I see that makeup? Did you do that yourself?"

Jessie's cheek twitched and she laughed, loud and shrill. The sound might have been cute coming from the mouth of a little girl playing *doll* on her father's lap, but as an adult splattered with gore, it stopped Catriona in her tracks.

"Makeup? This is just dirt from ropin' and ridin'."

Jessie's mouth snapped open and closed in time with the words, but her lips and cheek muscles remained frozen. She flicked her head to the right toward Fiona. "I roped me a good one here."

Fiona appeared in shock. Catriona could see how Jessie had cut her from the left corner of her mouth to her chin, simulating the hinges of her own painted dummy jaw.

The wound bled like any head wound. *Copiously*. Catriona felt confident that without distraction, Jessie would have mirrored her carving on the opposite side of Fiona's mouth to complete the effect.

Only a few feet from the foot of the stage, Catriona took another step forward. "You're a real cowgirl? You rope and ride?"

Jessie's attention snapped back to Catriona. "Do I? I'm Cassidy Cowgirl! That's what I do best!"

Reaching the edge of the stage, Catriona stopped, unable to walk any farther.

What do I do now?

She felt helpless on the ground, the floor of the stage hovering at her chest. Jessie had the advantage of high ground. She could jump from there, lunge, or simply stay away. If she turned to stab Fiona, Catriona would never be able to scramble onto the platform in time to stop her from inflicting more damage—even mortal damage.

Glancing in Fiona's direction, she spotted a flash of movement behind the actress.

Oh, you big beautiful beast.

Broch had made his way to the side of the stage and now stood behind Fiona. The chair had been placed at the very edge of the stage and his hands were wrapped around its legs.

She understood. He planned to jerk the chair off the stage, moving Fiona from Jessie's reach. But he couldn't do it with the large knife still pressed against the actress's throat. It was too risky.

Catriona smiled and locked her gaze on Jessie's.

You're right-handed. Please tell me I'm remembering this right...

"Hey, Cassidy!" called Catriona, trying to make her voice as light and childish as Jessie's.

Jessie's jaw dropped, the sides of her mouth curling ever-so-slightly. A ventriloquist dummy version of a smile.

Not cute.

Catriona had never liked dolls before and she suspected after today she'd never be able to sit in a room with one again.

Here goes nothing.

"Cassidy, can you circle the wagons?"

Jessie's eyes grew even wider.

"Can I circle the wagons?"

Jessie's right hand shot up in the air, her fingers still curled around the handle of the knife. She orbited it there, pantomiming an invisible lasso.

"Circle the wagons!"

The moment her hand left Fiona's throat, Broch jerked the chair, sending it and Fiona tumbling off the side of the stage.

Fiona screamed.

Jessie spun, her expression twisting into confusion at Fiona's disappearance. Spotting Broch, she froze.

"Drop the knife," commanded Catriona.

Jessie turned back to her. Catriona held her gun on her. She thought her weapon would be enough to hold Jessie's attention, but the girl's gaze immediately shot up and over Catriona's head.

"Drop the gun!" called a man's voice.

Catriona glanced over her shoulder. A police officer stood at the end of the aisle, his gun raised. She recognized him as the officer they'd left behind at Walker's house. He must have spotted the cars parked in front of the amusement park on his way home and stopped to investigate.

Jessie bolted left across the stage.

"Freeze! Drop it!" the cop's gun followed Jessie's path and then returned to Catriona.

Catriona held up her gun and then squatted to place it on

the ground.

"It's me. From Walker's place. She's the one that left the burned body," she called to the officer as she pointed after Jessie.

She stood. "I'm going to catch her."

She turned and ran after Jessie, praying the cop didn't fire.

"Freeze, both of you!" called the officer, but he didn't shoot.

"O'er 'ere! Ah hae an injured wummin!"

Catriona heard Broch's roar, grateful the Highlander had thought to distract the officer.

Jessie reached the end of the stage, sliding in her cowboy boots as she prepared to jump over the edge. She paused long enough for Catriona to catch up, paralleling the girl from her position on the ground.

Catriona tackled Jessie as she slid off the edge of the stage, doing her best to keep her attention trained on the girl's knife. As they tumbled, she grabbed Jessie's wrist and held it pinned to the ground. The cowgirl hit the ground chest-first with a great expelling of breath, giving Catriona the time to wrench her wrist behind her back.

Jessie howled with what sounded like fury.

"Drop the knife," said Catriona, as she strained to keep the thrashing suspect down.

Jessie released the weapon and Catriona grabbed it with her opposite hand to toss it away.

"I said *freeze*!"

Catriona turned. The officer stood a few feet from her, gun trained on her back.

"You remember me?" Catriona asked him.

He nodded. His eyes seemed frightened. She guessed he hadn't been long on the job.

"Let go of me," demanded Jessie, attempting to buck

Catriona from her back. She wasn't a large person, and Catriona pushed her back to the ground. She pulled the girl's arm a little tighter and Jessie squealed in pain.

The officer holstered his gun and pulled his cuffs from his side. He took Jessie's wrist from Catriona and cuffed her behind her back.

Jessie turned her head, revealing her face, and the officer gasped.

"I probably should have warned you about that," mumbled Catriona.

The officer pulled his radio from his shoulder and called for help.

EPILOGUE

Jessie Walker, as Cassidy Cowgirl, had no problem confessing her crimes to the police. She admitted she'd exacted revenge on Parasol's talent, which made Sean, Luther, and Catriona's lives easier.

Fiona had a harder time of it. She spent time in the hospital, where Catriona and Broch visited her. Catriona figured it might be the best time to coerce a little truth out of the witch.

Maybe the pain meds would help.

Catriona and Broch entered Fiona's hospital room, where she lay, eyes closed, with a bandage wrapped around her chin. Flowers from well-wishers choked her room. A tall, floor vase filled with three dozen roses stood like a sentry in the corner of the room. Drawn to it, Catriona smelled the flowers and found the card, turning it so she might read it.

"Get well soon, Raven-girl, all my love, *Aaron*," she read aloud.

"That's his nickname for me," mumbled a voice.

Catriona turned to find Fiona staring at her.

"I doubt you're supposed to be talking. I thought with your face wrapped up I'd have a chance to get a word in edge-wise."

Fiona chuckled and then grimaced as if in pain, hooking the left side of her mouth to murmur as best she could without moving the right. "One side's fine."

"Thanks to me."

Fiona acquiesced with a nod. Her eyes shifted to Broch.

"Remember me?" she asked.

He lifted his shirt to show her the scar on his abdomen—the one he'd arrived with.

"Ah remember ye."

The scar appeared even angrier than it had lately.

Catriona looked at Fiona, wondering if her proximity to Broch somehow aggravated it.

Catriona took a deep breath and prepared to launch into a speech about how she'd figured out Fiona's wicked game and how she wasn't going to put up with her meddling at the studio, but a tiny dark red dot on Broch's face caught her eye, robbing her of her concentration.

Mesmerized, she walked toward him.

He noticed her attention and scowled.

"Whit is it?'

She reached up and touched his forehead where the scar straddling his eye began. Looking at her finger, she found it red and wet.

"Your scar is bleeding."

"Whit?" Broch reached up and touched his face with the same result. He stared at the dab of blood on his fingertip.

His gaze shot to Fiona. "Ye did this tae?"

Catriona awaited her sister's answer. It seemed Broch had also worked out that Fiona's presence aggravated the wound she'd given him nearly two centuries earlier.

Fiona's gaze shifted to the left to peer past Broch.

Her eyes saucered.

Catriona followed her sister's attention to a tall, impossibly thin man standing in the hall. His eyes were such an icy blue they appeared white. He wore long sleeves and a leather glove over one hand.

Broch turned, and Catriona watched his jaw drop.

"Do you know him?" she asked.

Broch nodded, his attention locked on the man's glove.

"Who—?" Catriona turned to Fiona for answers.

The corners of Fiona's eyes crinkled as if she were trying to smile.

"Hi, Dad," she said.

~~ THE END ~~

WANT SOME MORE? FREE PREVIEWS!

If you liked this book, read on for a preview of the next Kilty AND the Shee McQueen Mystery-Thriller Series!

THANK YOU FOR READING!

If you enjoyed this book, please swing back to Amazon and **leave me a review** — even short reviews help authors like me find new fans! You can also FOLLOW AMY on AMAZON

ABOUT THE AUTHOR

USA Today and Wall Street Journal bestselling author Amy Vansant has written over 20 books, including the fun, thrilling Shee McQueen series, the rollicking, twisty Pineapple Port Mysteries, and the action-packed Kilty urban fantasies. Throw in a couple romances and a YA fantasy for her nieces...

Amy specializes in fun, exciting reads with plenty of laughs and action -- she tried to write serious books, but they always ended up full of jokes, so she gave up.

Amy lives in Jupiter, Florida with her muse/husband a goony Bordoodle named Archer.

Books by Amy Vansant

Pineapple Port Mysteries
Funny, clean & full of unforgettable characters

Shee McQueen Mystery-Thrillers
Action-packed, fun romantic mystery-thrillers

Kilty Urban Fantasy/Romantic Suspense
Action-packed romantic suspense/urban fantasy

Slightly Romantic Comedies
Classic romantic romps

The Magicatory
Middle-grade fantasy

FREE PREVIEW

KILTY AS SIN

CHAPTER ONE

Six Months Ago

Peter felt the man before he saw him.

He, his buddy Dean and their boss, Volkov, sat stage-side at the Minty Minx strip club, watching a sleepy-eyed redhead loll through her pole routine. It wouldn't have surprised Peter if she'd stopped to check her text messages in the middle of the dance. Though, he couldn't imagine where she'd keep her phone.

A redheaded stripper named *Ginger*. She hadn't shown any effort in picking a stage name, either.

Nothing kept Dean from checking his phone. He'd been texting back and forth with someone since they arrived. Volkov only had eyes for Ginger. Peter spent half his time watching the girl and the other half staring at the wall opposite her. Dean had found Peter the job with Volkov only a few days earlier, so Peter felt obligated to look grateful for the free trip to the strip joint.

In truth, it wasn't his thing.

The job paid well—Volkov was some kind of Russian gangster, although Dean said he wasn't connected to the real Russian mob—he was a lone wolf. Dean said that was funny because that's what Volkov's name meant. *Wolf*.

Dean had implied it was the mob who didn't want Volkov and not the other way around, but Peter didn't care. He was a bit of a Russian mutt, on his mother's side.

The job had come just in time. Peter needed the money. He'd done three months in High Desert State Prison for drug possession with intent to distribute—though he'd had no intent to sell. The meth was all for him.

He got clean in prison and, following his early release for good behavior, Dean said he could take over *his* job. The position watching over Volkov's safe house came with room and board, so it solved all of Peter's post-prison problems.

Dean packed up and moved out of Volkov's safe house two seconds after Peter walked through the door. "Good luck," he'd said. Peter hadn't loved his tone, or the little chuckle that followed, but he figured, *how bad could it be?*

Free rent was free rent.

His gaze following Ginger's travels down the pole, Dean stood and slipped his phone back into his pocket. He slapped Volkov on the back and said something to him. Volkov nodded, his attention never leaving Ginger.

A quick nod to Peter and Dean left. Peter glanced at Volkov. It seemed they'd be staying.

Peter returned to watching Ginger rub her cheek against the pole. Not her rear cheeks, but her *face* cheek. It hit him as odd. He suspected she was trying to grab a quick nap.

That's when he *felt* a presence in the chair left empty by Dean's absence. He turned, thinking Dean had returned, but it wasn't his buddy. The man sitting between them now was taller and thinner.

The man glanced in his direction, revealing eyes so light blue they looked white. A black edge rimmed the man's pale irises but Peter only caught a brief glimpse. The man looked away as if Peter wasn't worth considering.

Dick.

Volkov and the stranger talked. From the bits and pieces Peter overheard, he couldn't tell if the two men knew each other or not.

"I like to take them home," Volkov screamed over the

throbbing music.

"It would be nice to keep them and pull them out when you want a dance, huh?" said the man.

Peter looked at White-Eyes, expecting him to be chuckling at his stupid joke, but he wasn't. He stared at Ginger with those crazy eyes. Serious as cancer.

Something made Peter's neck shiver and he bunched his shoulders against the cold.

"It's harder than you think," said Volkov, laughing.

Peter relaxed a little. The fact Volkov laughed made everything seem more normal.

Except...

He'd been at Volkov's safe house for two nights. Someone had torn out the main bathroom and refashioned it as an empty, windowless, oversized closet. The room gave Peter the creeps, both because it reminded him of his cell back at High Desert and because it wasn't *right*. He'd asked Dean what it was for and Dean said, "It's Volkov's. You want the job or not?"

So, he'd let it drop.

"Basements make good sound dampeners."

Peter looked at White-Eyes again.

What did he just say?

Peter couldn't shake the uneasiness creeping along his scalp. He was no women's libber—he'd made his share of off-color jokes. But something about the way Volkov and White-Eyes were talking about captive women—it sounded more like a scientific discussion than fantasy banter.

It sounded like a *plan*.

Peter concentrated on Ginger's freckled breasts, but a sudden, inexplicable vision of himself digging a basement through the hard Nevada caliche filled his brain. He had an abrupt urge to leap up, buy pickaxes and shovels, and start digging.

For Ginger.

As he watched the girl sway to the music, Peter realized he wanted to put *Ginger* in the hole.

Not any hole.

The hole *he* dug.

Peter rubbed his hand across his head as if he were trying to raise a genie from his skull.

What the hell is wrong with me?

He'd never had thoughts like that in his life.

Peter felt a movement at his elbow and turned to see White-Eyes standing to leave.

Thank God.

As the thin man moved away, he banged into Peter with his right arm. His flesh was hard. It felt as though someone had bumped into him with a bat.

Peter glanced at Volkov. The Russian watched Ginger.

Peter did the same.

After a bit, he felt better. He pushed the image of himself digging holes from his mind and watched Volkov hand Ginger a stack of money. Not stripper money. *Real money.* Ginger nodded, talking with Volkov.

Peter couldn't hear what they were talking about.

It didn't hit him as odd when he found himself driving Volkov and Ginger back to the safe house. He'd hoped he'd be dropping the two of them off at Volkov's real house, but the Russian had muttered the address of the safe house to him as he and the girl slid into the backseat.

Peter heard the two of them mumbling as he drove. Ginger wasn't a giggler. Her personality didn't perk *off* stage, either.

When they arrived at the safe house, Ginger wandered into the kitchen muttering something about sparkling water.

'Cause she's so fancy.

Volkov opened the linen closet and pulled out a black tote bag Peter had never noticed before. Volkov took the bag into the cell room, before leading the girl to the bag and shutting the door behind them.

Peter stood there, staring at the closed door, unsure what he was supposed to do while his boss had sex in a jail cell with a stripper. On either side of the cell room were bedrooms. Why would he take her into the empty cell?

When the screaming started, Peter turned up the television and sat on the sofa. The walls of the cell were hard, like cement, and the door had been reinforced with strips of thick wood, but Peter still heard the screaming.

It didn't sound like sex screaming.

Every so often the door would rattle as if someone had thrown themselves against it.

Peter turned up the volume again. After another ten minutes, he grabbed a bottle of vodka from the kitchen. He wasn't supposed to drink, but...it's not like it was *meth*. He poured himself a large shot and then another.

Peter carried the bottle back to the sofa.

Peter opened his eyes. He'd fallen asleep. He looked at the cell door to find it cracked open.

"Volkov?"

He must have left.

The bottle of vodka sitting on the table beside him was nearly empty. Was he supposed to be keeping watch?

I hope I'm not in trouble.

Peter turned down the television and stood, staring at the cell door. He crossed the four feet to the entrance and was about to peek inside when the door swung open. Ginger stumbled past, pushing him, nearly knocking him over on her way toward the front door. Her face was swollen and covered in blood.

She pushed open the screen door and ran out of the house, screaming. A second later Peter heard the screeching of tires and a thump.

The screaming stopped.

"Go see."

Peter jumped. Volkov stood behind him, his body naked but for a pair of wrestling shorts, his tattooed skin glistening with sweat and blood.

"What?" he asked. His mind felt like a seized motor.

Volkov grabbed and squeezed his arm before pushing him toward the front door. *"Go find her."*

Peter followed in Ginger's footsteps. People gathered on the road outside the house. A man stood over the form of a red-headed girl, her twisted body illuminated in the headlights of his Impala.

Ginger's left leg bent at an unnatural angle. Her body was covered in scrapes. She wasn't naked, which struck Peter as the oddest thing of all.

"She came out of nowhere." The man hovering over her repeated the phrase over and over. People around them announced they were calling 911.

Peter turned and reentered the house. He found his boss in the cell room.

Volkov had thrown on one of Peter's t-shirts. In his hand hung a bucket, an orange sponge floating in the murky water. The room looked as it always did, but for the smell of disinfectant.

Volkov thrust the bucket at him. "Dump this down the sink and put the bucket underneath."

Peter took the bucket and did as he was told. The water appeared light red against the white sink as it swirled down the drain.

When he returned to the living room, Volkov tossed his t-shirt at him. He had slipped back into the black oxford he'd been wearing at the club.

"I wasn't here," said the Russian.

Peter nodded.

Volkov pushed past him, walking through the kitchen toward the back door, pausing on the porch off the back. He tapped his toe on the ground and then looked back at Peter.

"Tomorrow go out and get some shovels and pickaxes.

Things to dig."

Peter nodded.

"Puttin' in a pool?" he asked.

He wasn't sure why he'd said it.

He knew they wouldn't be digging a pool.

Get *Kilty As Sin* on Amazon!

ANOTHER FREE PREVIEW!

THE GIRL WHO WANTS

A Shee McQueen Mystery-Thriller by Amy Vansant

Chapter One

Three Weeks Ago, Nashua, New Hampshire.

Shee realized her mistake the moment her feet left the grass.
He's enormous.

She'd watched him drop from the side window of the house. He landed four feet from where she stood, and still, her brain refused to register the warning signs. The nose, big and lumpy as breadfruit, the forehead some beach town could use as a jetty if they buried him to his neck...

His knees bent to absorb his weight and *her* brain thought, *got you.*

Her brain couldn't be bothered with simple math: *Giant, plus Shee, equals Pain.*

Instead, she jumped to tackle him, dangling airborne as his knees straightened and the *pet the rabbit* bastard stood to his full height.

Crap.

The math added up pretty quickly after that.

Hovering like Superman mid-flight, there wasn't much she could do to change her disastrous trajectory. She'd *felt* like a superhero when she left the ground. Now, she felt more like a Canada goose staring into the propellers of Captain Sully's Airbus A320.

She might take down the plane, but it was going to *hurt.*

Frankenjerk turned toward her at the same moment she plowed into him. She clamped her arms around his waist like a little girl hugging a redwood. Lurch returned the embrace, twisting her to the ground. Her back hit the dirt and air burst from her lungs like a double shotgun blast.

Ow.

Wheezing, she punched upward, striking Beardless Hagrid in the throat.

That didn't go over well.

Grabbing her shoulder with one hand, Dickasaurus flipped her on her stomach like a sausage link, slipped his hand under her chin and pressed his forearm against her windpipe.

The only air she'd gulped before he cut her supply stank of damp armpit. He'd tucked her cranium in his arm crotch, much like the famous noggin-less horseman once held his severed head. Fireworks exploded in the dark behind her eyes.

That's when a thought occurred to her.

I haven't been home in fifteen years.

What if she died in Gigantor's armpit? Would her father even know?

Has it really been that long?

Flopping like a landed fish, she forced her assailant to adjust his hold and sucked a breath as she flipped on her back. Spittle glistened on his lips, his brow furrowed as if she'd asked him to read a paragraph of big-boy words.

His nostrils flared like the Holland Tunnel.

There's an idea.

Making a V with her fingers, Shee thrust upward, stabbing into his nose, straining to reach his tiny brain.

Goliath roared. Jerking back, he grabbed her arm to unplug her fingers from his nose socket. She whipped away her limb before he had a good grip, fearing he'd snap her bones with his Godzilla paws.

Kneeling before her, he clamped both hands over his face, cursing as blood seeped from behind his fingers.

Shee's gaze didn't linger on that mess. Her focus fell to his crotch, hovering a foot above her feet, protected by nothing but a thin pair of oversized sweatpants.

Scrambled eggs, sir?

She kicked.

He howled.

Shee scuttled back like a crab, found her feet and snatched her gun from her side. The gun she should have pulled *before* trying to tackle the Empire State Building.

"Move a muscle and I'll aerate you," she said. She always liked that line.

The golem growled, but remained on the ground like a good dog, cradling his family jewels.

Shee's partner in this manhunt, a local cop easier on the eyes than he was useful, rounded the corner and drew his own weapon.

She smiled and holstered the gun he'd lent her.

Unknowingly.

"Glad you could make it."

Her portion of the operation accomplished, she headed toward the car as more officers swarmed the scene.

"Shee, where are you going?" called the cop.

She stopped and turned.

"Home, I think."

His gaze dropped to her hip.

"Is that my gun?"

Get *The Girl Who Wants* on Amazon!

ISBN-9781720025283
Library of Congress: 2018908982

Vansant Creations, LLC / Amy Vansant
Jupiter, FL

http://www.AmyVansant.com

Copy editing by Carolyn Steele
Proofreading by Effrosyni Moschoudi, Meg Barnhart &
Connie Leap
Cover by Lance Buckley & Amy Vansant

Made in United States
North Haven, CT
01 July 2024

54302736R00137